Medical Adventures of Sherlock Holmes, Dr. Watson, and Dr. Verner

Carl L. Heifetz

Paperback ISBN 978-1-78705-310-6
ePub ISBN 978-1-78705-311-3
PDF ISBN 978-1-78705-312-0

Published in the UK by MX Publishing
335 Princess Park Manor, Royal Drive,
London, N11 3GX
www.mxpublishing.com

Cover layout and construction by
Brian Belanger

Contents

To Sandie, thanks for all your
support in editing these stories

Dr. Verner and the Mysterious Oriental Disease

The leaders of the Verner clan that inhabit their secret business empire, headquartered in a line of warehouses that dot the Detroit River, were just wrapping up their weekly executive meeting. The attendees were the titular head, Uncle Horace Vernet, his wife Juliet, his heir apparent and nephew Maurice Verner, and Maurice's beautiful blonde wife Alicia. Their businesses had been going very well in their various independent enterprises, and they had concluded their discussion early. They strolled over to the special Sherlock Holmes sitting room that had been brought over from Baker Street in London, England, and sat down in the ancient chairs imported over three generations ago. After dispensing some of the contents of the Tantalus and gasogene, Maurice removed the prized, secret narratives of Dr. Watson from the hidden recesses in their antique roll top desk.

Maurice said, "I'm about to read aloud from the sacred text of one of Dr. Watson's adventures with our English forbear Dr. Maurice Verner. In this account, Dr. Verner uses his medical skills as a bacteriological researcher to solve another deadly infection with the assistance of Dr. Watson. Together, they saved the life of an infected girl, prevented the spread of the unknown disease to workers in the fabric industry, and captured the evil and malevolent villain responsible. Dr. Watson entitled it 'Dr. Verner and the Mysterious Oriental Disease.' "
Dr. Watson's narrative commences:

The dual horror of Sherlock Holmes' untimely death in the Reichenbach Falls and the demise of my sweet wife Mary, from pneumonia, have begun to diminish dual deleterious effects on my consciousness. Relieved of the need to keep busy with my medical practice and research, I have decided to slow my pace. I intend to turn my attention to writing additional exciting episodes of my previous adventures with Sherlock Holmes. My recent excursion to Coombe Tracey and the murders involved with the "pearls of death" spurred my interests in mentally returning to previous events in Dartmoor. As I was starting to organize my thoughts to write the tale of the giant dog that hounded the Baskerville family for several generations, the case that is the subject of this narrative intervened.

The tall 30-something woman who accompanied my friend Maurice Verner was strikingly beautiful. He introduced her as Jeannine Lafarge, his fiancée. The slight trill in her voice indicted that she was a Francophone, although she spoke English with very little French accent. Her long black hair and loose fitting solid red gown indicated that she had Bohemian instincts. I quickly noted that she was an independent woman from her firm hand shake and direct, frank look in her dark brown eyes. The roughly edged and slightly pigmented finger tips alerted me to the fact that she was a member of the arts community.

My deduction was affirmed when Maurice said, "Jeannine is a good friend of my cousins, the artists of the French Vernets. I was introduced to her in my recent two-month visit to Paris where I met Mr. Louis Pasteur. She accompanied me to Montpellier where I attended seminars at the famous medical school, and in Berlin where I visited the immunology researcher Paul Ehrlich. Jeannine is a designer of fabrics for wall hangings and upholstered furniture. She also is known for her oil paintings and watercolors. She has relocated to London as an artist-in-residence at a noted design studio. We will plan our wedding for several months hence. I would greatly appreciate it if you would stand by me during the ceremony. I hope that you are not adverse to an Anglican ritual. We are both French Protestants, and are accustomed to the related ceremonies of the Church of England."

I replied, "I would be proud to stand by you at your nuptials. I am a Protestant myself, being a Presbyterian from Scotland originally."

"Then all is settled," replied Maurice. "All I will need is to find accommodations where my wife and I can reside as a married couple. I don't think our current bachelor establishment would be appropriate."

As Maurice led Jeannine up the stairs, carrying their luggage, he stated, "I'm giving my future bride a tour of our surgical suites and my laboratory, and then I will get her settled in her hotel. Would you like to meet us at the Langdon Hotel for dinner at eight? I will pick you up at half past seven."

I happily assented. As they climbed the stairs holding hands, they displayed the energy of their youth and their early stages of love. It reminded me of my romance with Mary Morstan and made me yearn for her presence. Then I began to think about my future living arrangements. Without a wife or apartment-mate, the large quarters would be very empty and lonely. I closed my eyes and recalled the many fulfilled months that I spent with Sherlock Holmes.

During the weeks that slowly passed, I saw very little of Maurice. He attended to his patients when he was in the physician's offices. Also, he pursued his bacteriological research, perfecting the technology he had learned on the continent. And, he spent a great deal of time getting Jeannine settled in her career and a permanent location of residence.

Meanwhile, I finally started on my story regarding the exciting activities on the dangerous moor. The enforced quiet was rudely broken during a summer afternoon. My surgery was empty, and I had spent several quiet hours after lunch working on my writing. Maurice was busily performing experiments, and Billy was straightening my examining room for several late afternoon appointments.

Suddenly I heard Billy's piping voice shrieking, "Dr. Watson, there is an emergency."

Then, lightly trotting up the stairs were female footsteps. It was Jeannine. She yelled in her contralto voice, "Dr. Watson, please get Maurice. My assistant Janice is very ill and needs help."

I carried the young woman in my arms and limped running up the stairs to Maurice's facility. Billy preceded me, threw open the door and yelled "Dr. Verner, help! A girl is sick. She is being carried up by Dr. Watson! Your lady friend is with them."

Maurice, his face flushed with fear said, "Is Jeannine all right?"

"Yes," I replied, "It's one of her workers, a young lady. Where should I put her?"

Pointing at his steel examining table, Maurice quickly wiped it down with isopropanol and laid a cloth on its surface. He said, "Deposit her here."

Then turning to Jeannine he asked, "Who is it and what's wrong?"

"It's one of my workers, a girl named Janice. She looks like she has a serious infection. Her left hand is all swollen and bears abscesses."

Maurice turned to me and said, "James, check her pulse, breath sounds, and temperature."

As I performed the standard examination, Maurice looked at Jeannine and said, "As a woman, I need you to disrobe the girl and feel around for signs of swelling. Is she conscious? If so, talk to her and see if she is in pain."

After my perfunctory exam, I said, "Her pulse is very weak and her blood pressure is very low. I think she is going into shock.

Jeannine added, "There are no additional signs of sickness. Her breathing is normal and she said that the only pain is in her swollen hand. "

I followed with an assessment of her blood pressure. I said, "Her pressure is now normal as are her heart sounds. She is on the way to recovery."

Maurice stretched out her hand and, using a needle and syringe, withdrew a sample of white, milky purulent material from the abscesses. He inoculated liquid and solid yellowish bacteriological culture media with specimens, and prepared microscopic slides. He fixed the specimens on the slides with gentle heat from a Bunsen flame. He then performed a complex staining procedure with a violet colored liquid, washing the surface with alcohol, and then counterstaining with a red liquid.

He said, "This is a new procedure that was invented by Christian Gram. It bears his name."

Looking at the slide through his high power microscope, Maurice announced "This is a Gram Negative rod shaped bacterium. Note the red color. Gram Positive microbes retain the violet color of the initial stain. And note the shape. It appears like safety pins, hollowed out in the middle. I know exactly what it is. It's Tapanuli Fever. Look at it."

I looked at the unusual shape. Then I asked with surprise, "How did you know about the bacterium and what it looks like?"

"James, you brought it to my attention when you told me the story about Sherlock Holmes' feigned sickness. After you told me, I knew that I needed to acquire the microbial collection belonging to Culverton Smith. His heirs were very happy to rid themselves of the dangerous items, and I was happy to add his microbes, culture media, and notes to my collection. I dreaded the thought that such hazardous bacteria could get into people's hands. Just think how dangerous they would be if treacherous enemies learned about them. I did of, course, get permission from cousin Mycroft since they would be considered as evidence in a criminal case."

"What are you planning to do next?" I inquired.

"Please watch her carefully for signs of continuing illness. Cut open the abscess with a sterile blade, remove the pus, wipe the blood with alcohol, and carefully apply sterile bandages. I have already prepared, in my research, rabbit antiserum using the methods that I learned in Mr. Pasteur's laboratory."

Maurice removed a flask from the refrigerator. The vessel contained a yellow fluid. Maurice used a large syringe and needle to administer about a dram of the liquid intravenously.

"How did you prepare the serum?" I asked.

Maurice explained, "I grew the bacteria from Culverton Smith's laboratory in the culture media that he had developed. Then I killed the culture with heat and injected the dead microbes in rabbits. I removed the blood from the animals and prepared pure serum. I'm hoping that Smith's culture is identical to the one that I used to prepare the serum."

Then I inquired, "How did you know that the serum would be effective?"

He replied, "I infected mice with living bacteria. Then I was able to cure the infection with intravenous injection of the antiserum. I'm hoping that we would never require it in a warfare situation, but in the case of this young woman, the antiserum might save her life. I'm stepping down to the street to send a telegram to my laboratory at Bart's to get a fresh supply I have just tested for sterility and effectiveness."

As Jeannine comforted the young woman by stroking her hand, the girl slowly recovered her health. By the time Maurice had the additional antiserum in hand, the patient was well on the way to recovery.

I asked Maurice, "If I recall what Holmes had told me, when Smith's relative was administered the bacterium, he died within days. Why is our patient recovering?"

Maurice replied, "In my laboratory experiments in mice, the pathogenesis of the infection depends on the size of the infectious dose and the route of administration. When introduced intravenously, the mice died within two to three days. When intraperitoneal doses were administered, it took weeks to kill the animal. Intradermal dosing rarely resulted in death, although some sickness developed. Fortunately, in the case of Janice, I think that's her name, she only received a cutaneous inoculation. That is the least infectious mode of administration source. We are lucky that this villain did not know how to administer the microbe for the most effect. Thus, he was not an expert.

Glancing at my watch, I realized that I needed to be off for two patients whom I promised to call on after tea time. After telling Maurice that I had to leave, he scribbled a note for me to obtain a messenger to take it to St. Bart's. As I left, I acquired the services of a commissionaire for the task, and then jumped into a Hansom to visit my patients. My afternoon tea would have to wait.

Returning in an hour, the aura in Maurice's surgical suite had greatly improved. Janice was sitting up in a wooden chair eating soup from a bowl on the table. She was smiling, and looked at me gratefully. Her left hand was freshly dressed and bandaged.

Jeannine, who was gently stroking her back, arose and said, "As soon as Dr. Verner's intern and nurse arrive with more serum and sterile dressings, we can leave to investigate the source of this infection."

After greeting his associates, Maurice turned to me and said, "Janice will be well cared for. It appears that the serum ameliorated the infection, but I intend to administer additional doses and have the wound checked for further response. Also, I will need to prepare more serum just in case the strain that infected Janice was not identical to the vaccine isolate. A visiting nurse will join Janice with fresh clothes and to spend the night with her. It is time for us to cease being doctors and to follow our detective instincts. I'm bringing Jeannine along with us since she knows her way around the factory in which Janice works. We must find out how Janice received the infection, why it was done, and bring the miscreant to justice. It has become a government case since I'm troubled by the likelihood that enemies of the crown would adapt this disease to warfare. Our old friend Mr. Melas will assist us. Oh, don't forget to load your revolver. Anyone who would attempt to murder someone should be considered dangerous."

As three of us exited my offices, we were met with the same official government coach that we had used in our previous services for the state. It was a closed carriage drawn by two large steeds. There was no conversation since Jeannine and Maurice were quietly gazing in each other's eyes and holding hands. It reminded me of my first encounter with my dear wife Mary. The warmth of the afternoon sun and the quiet of the carriage interior conspired to render me asleep. Thus, when Maurice's gentle nudge on my shoulder awakened me, I had no idea where we were in London. It was obviously a newly minted commercial district with several large rectangular buildings. Smoke emanated from the chimneys, windows expelled steam, and there was the sound of pumps and pistons churning out powerful activity. The sight of Mr. Melas awaiting us in front of a large green sign with white letters denoting 'Archibald and Son's Fabrics' indicated the termination of our journey. After introducing Jeannine and Melas to one another, the former escorted us into the facility and led us up two flights of stairs to a large dimly lit hallway bounded by rows of gray doors.

Jeannine pointed to a door on the right and beckoned for us to enter. Melas led the way into a large room with six large tables on both walls. Seated at each table was a middle aged, gray-haired woman sewing indigo-colored fabrics into what appeared to be covers for chairs. Two young boys were picking up completed projects and distributing additional bundles of cloth and spools of matching thread. Only one table was not in use. That was obviously Janice's station.

Jeannine spoke first. Addressing us, she stated, "These are the ladies who work with me on new designs for fabrics to make wall hangings, table covers, and upholstery. They are my most competent employees. Janice has recently been elevated to assist them."

Then, turning to the women, Jeannine addressed her workers. "Ladies," she said, "You will note that Janice is not here today. She has taken ill and has a serious infection. She has been taken care of by Dr. Watson and Dr. Verner over here. Janice is now recovering nicely and should be back at work soon. Are any of you feeling ill?"

Only one woman responded, "I do have a cold, but otherwise I feel fine."

Then Jeannine continued, "Did any of you notice when Janice became sick?"

"The same woman, who appeared to be their spokesperson responded in a nasal voice, "Janice did complain about her hand being sore and swollen. You know how these young folks are. They can't stand hard work. When we came back from lunch, she was gone. Is she contagious?

Maurice responded, "She is not contagious. But I need to ask some questions so I can try to determine the cause of her illness and if any of you are at risk before you can return to work."

Another woman said, "We get paid by the piece. We can't afford to slack off."

Jeannine smiled and said, "Ladies, you will be paid a full day's wages. In fact, I'll double it. Is that satisfactory?"

They all nodded their agreement.

Turning to Jeannine, Maurice said, "Please show me the procedure that each worker uses from the beginning of the shift."

Jeannine motioned for each woman to take everything off of her table. She then called the two boys over and ordered, "Set up the tables as you did in the morning.'

The youths put a pile of fabric and spindle of matching thread on each table. The ladies then reached into their pockets in their smocks and each one put a thimble on the table in front of her. Only Janice's station remained untouched.

Maurice asked, "What do you do next?"

Jeannine nodded for the women to continue. Each took the end of the thread, wetted it in her mouth, and threaded her needle. Then each put a thimble on her left hand and screwed it on her index finger tightly. Then picking up the cloth, they began to stitch it into a pattern."

Maurice asked, "Where do you get the thimbles?"

The same spokeswoman responded, "From the blonde boy, Teddy, when we first arrive. We use the same thimble all day."

"Thank you, ladies. Did Janice do anything different?" asked Maurice.

In tandem, all of the women shook their heads and continued their work.

Then Maurice asked Jeannine, "I notice that the fabric on Janice's station is a much deeper color indigo than the other fabrics, which appear to be identical with each other."

Jeannine replied, "You have a good eye for color. It must be something that you inherited from your artistic family. Janice's fabric is dyed with a new synthetic indigo whereas the others are the traditionally colored fabric using naturally existing indigo pigment. We are experimenting with the coal-tar derived dye. It's much brighter than the natural substance, more uniform in color, and much less expensive. We wanted the experienced workers to use the standard fabric since we need them to finish as quickly as possible. If Janice has a problem with her job, we would not lose production time."

"Is Janice the only person working with the new fabric?" asked Maurice.

"Yes, she is. As our newest employee, we didn't want to put a critical production batch at risk. We left the critical batches in the hands of more experienced employees."

Then Maurice picked up the thimble that still resided on Janice's station. He then addressed the ladies, "We will need each of you to receive a medical exam." As a small woman in a white cap arrived he stated, "Please follow this nurse to the waiting coach outside for a ride to St. Bart's. After she checks your hand, we will provide transportation to your homes."

At that declaration, the nurse led them through the door and escorted the workers to the exit. Then, Maurice gathered their thimbles, making certain to identify them with a wax marker.

After we arrived at my offices, Maurice scribbled a list on a prescription pad and asked Mr. Melas to deliver the items to Jeannine's establishment by six o'clock that afternoon. Maurice then summoned Billy.

While Billy was waiting for his orders, Maurice said to Jeannie, "How many purveyors are there for indigo dye?"

Jeannine responded, "There are only four in London."

Maurice tore four sheets of paper from his prescription pad, and wrote a note on each one. He then said to Jeannine, "Please write the name and address of the establishments on each of these."

He then turned to Billy and said, "Please deliver these. Here is a five-pound note to cover the transportation and the remainder for you."

Happy to be receiving a nice remittance, Billy smiled and began whistling as he descended the stairs.

Maurice addressed me and said, "James. I will require your assistance at eight o'clock at Jeannine's facility. Before you go about your business, let's check Janice's dressing and lesion. Then we can have lunch."

Janice was happily ensconced in Maurice's waiting room. She was smiling and appeared fully recovered. She was drawing dress designs in a note book that Jeannine had supplied. We were satisfied that her hand was well on the way to recovery, and we washed and redressed her finger. Her vital signs were all within reasonable limits.

Taking Janice's hand and smiling at the young woman, Jeannine gently escorted her down to the dining room while Maurice ran down to request a light supper. Janice showed an excellent appetite, as we all enjoyed the chips and kidney pie.

Then, we went about our business. Jeannine worked with Janice on her drawing skills; I recorded patient's notes and checked my calendar. Maurice sub-cultured his isolates, and then washed out each thimble into bacteriological media to determine if any had been inoculated with the dangerous microbe that had been the subject of our investigation. At five-thirty, Maurice stopped in to my office and told me that he had an errand. I was to meet him no later than eight p.m. with Jeannine, a police inspector and two constables. He left before I could inquire regarding our activities that evening. Maurice was getting more and more like Sherlock Holmes.

Using our newly installed telephone, I was able to arrange for Mr. Gregson and two constables to meet us at Jeannine's facility. At first, Gregson was hesitant, but the name Dr. Verner seemed to carry more weight than mine.

Traveling in a closed coach that had been delivered with the policemen, Jeannine and I joined the officers of the law on our journey. Janice had been left in the custody of Maurice's physician assistant and his nurse.

When we arrived at 'Archibald and Son's Fabrics,' the sky was moonless and dark. The closest gas light was several buildings distant. Using a small electric torch, Gregson tenuously led us to the barely visible door.

We were greeted at the open door by Melas who put his finger to his lips signaling that we were required to be silent. At Melas' hand signal, Gregson extinguished the light. In single file, we quietly ascended the stairs carefully, holding on to each other's hand.

As we arrived at the landing, Maurice whispered, "We may have a long wait. It is essential that we remain quiet and leaning on the wall."

The enforced vigil reminded me of my recent adventure with Sherlock Holmes when we thwarted the robbery of The City and Suburban Bank. However, our wait was not as long, and ended in most exciting way. The quiet was broken by footsteps scuttling up the stairs. And then they were directed into the room in which we were ensconced. It was obvious that the intruder knew his way into the appropriate chamber.

I was then shocked by a bright flashing light from the ceiling and a bell ringing. Then a male voice screamed in pain. The lights over the work tables were brightly illuminated to reveal a man attempting to extract his hand from a cabinet in the wall.

The man yelled in a high pitched voice, "Help! Let me go. The pain is terrible."

Maurice responded, "The pain that you feel is the bacteria attempting to penetrate your skin. Are you familiar with Tapanuli Fever? If you tell me who you are, I will release you. I'm a doctor and can help you."

The man gasped, "Please release me. My name is Jonathan Smith. I'm the son of Culverton Smith, the bacteriologist. Let me go and I'll tell you everything. I don't want to die for 500 pounds."

With that, Maurice pulled a copper wire from the recess and the blinking light and piercing sound ceased, and the man stopped moaning in pain. Maurice said, "I have disconnected you from the 50-volt battery. Tell me everything and I will remove the bacteriological trap."

The man responded, "I'm working for James Montgomery."

Jeannine, who had previously been silent, said menacingly, "He's one of the men that we purchase dyes from. He probably is trying to stop us from using synthetic indigo."

"Yes, that's correct," the man responded. "He recently purchased a huge supply of natural indigo, and doesn't want to lose the sale. He wanted to make it appear that the synthetic indigo was hazardous."

"So for commercial reasons, he attempted to take the life of a young worker. He should be ashamed of himself."

The young Smith countered, "He threatened my life. I had no choice. I work here and have custody of the thimbles. I had the inoculated one placed on the desk with the synthetic dye the day before. Don't blame the boys. They were just following orders. But the note that we received said that the girl had died, and that the employee had evidence regarding her murder. I hope that she was not killed."

Maurice turned to Inspector Gregson and Mr. Melas and asked, "Have you gentlemen heard enough? Can you take it from here?"

Melas responded, "I think that we have enough evidence to send them to prison, if not the noose. But do I understand that the mere threat of having evidence in the murder of the girl was enough to frighten them into action?"

"Yes," replied Maurice. "If you are going to murder someone, it's good to have experienced associates. I'm certain that Professor Moriarty would not have responded in such a manner. Also, I knew that the attempted murderer had no knowledge of the bacteria. Culverton Smith would have arranged for the bacteria to be injected. Now I will disassemble all of the rest of the painful and false injection. My electric device was wired to a 50-volt battery shocking the villain and signaling his presence. Additional pain was inflicted by tincture of cantharides glued to the paper with gum acacia."

With that, Maurice peeled the paper off of Jonathan Smith's hand and rinsed it off with a sponge of water that he had prepared for the occasion. The relieved man was placed in handcuffs and led away by Inspector Gregson.

Maurice said, "I think that we deserve a nice round of drinks. Let's pick up Janice and escort her to a fine restaurant of her choice.

Dr. Verner and the Secret Plague

After their very successful launch party for the latest romance novel penned by Juliet Vernet, under her *nom de plume* Veronica McPhair, some of the leading members of the Verner family retired to their secret Sherlock Holmes suite for a final nightcap before retiring for the evening. The event had lasted well into the night, and these several parties had decided to spend the night in their secure headquarters in their warehouse complex along the Detroit River. Since they had no activities planned for the following day, a Sunday, they had agreed to sleep late and then enjoy a delicious brunch at the nearby Rattlesnake Club before going to their private homes in the Detroit suburbs. The attendees were the titular head of the clan, Uncle Horace Vernet, his wife Juliet, his heir apparent and nephew Maurice Verner, and Maurice's beautiful blonde wife Alicia. They were also joined by Maurice's sister Evangeline and her new husband, Jacob Greene.

After distributing their alcoholic beverages of choice, Jacob said, "I have never been privileged to enter this room. I understand that you have a book of previously unpublished narratives written by Dr. Watson. May I read them?"

"Maurice, hand the booklet to Jacob. Let him do the honors," said Uncle Horace.

"This is about the first case with our ancestor Dr. Maurice Verner, after Sherlock Holmes returned from his supposed death in the Reichenbach Falls," said Maurice. "You can read it to us."

Jacob replied, "I was not aware that Sherlock Holmes had been thought dead."

Juliet replied with a chuckle, "If you are going to be one of us, you should read the stories edited by Dr. Arthur Conan Doyle. I'll give you the latest compendium containing the annotations by Mr. Leslie Klinger. You

16

might also enjoy the earlier annotation by Mr. Baring-Gould. Once you have read those, then you might like to read the accounts written by Dr. Watson of the adventures he shared with Dr. Verner during Sherlock Holmes' absence. However, since we have this volume in hand, it wouldn't hurt to start with that. But please, do not breathe a word of the Verner adventures. This compilation must never leave this room. Our ancestor never wanted his secretive nature revealed. Remember, everything our family does as a collective is top secret and can only be discussed amongst us. I'm certain that this was all explained to you and which you swore to before marrying Evangeline."

"Of course," responded Jacob. "My word is my sacred oath."

With that, he opened the loose leaf book to an item titled 'Dr. Verner and the Secret Plague.' He commenced narrating:

Dr. Maurice Verner looked up from the dead male figure that was splayed, in the nude, on his autopsy table in his laboratory. The deceased subject had bright red hair and blue eyes. He was roughly five and one-half feet in height and well nourished, but not quite plump. His most striking feature was a large blue inguinal swelling. There was no question in my mind concerning his cause of death.

Maurice looked at me, saying, "James, I don't know why you brought this case to my attention. It is clearly a death due to the bubonic plague. A microscopic analysis is not required since the sign of the infected lymph nodes are clearly diagnostic. However, I will perform a complete detailed necropsy if you insist, including microscopic evaluation of the lesions and culture of the contents. I will use this opportunity to add to my collection of specimens, since there have been very few reported studies with this organism. However, its clinical signs have been known since the time of the emperor Justinian, and have been described in millions of sufferers. Although somewhat uncommon in modern times, the disease has been experienced in habitats containing infected animals. The endemic location is in the forests and other wild areas. The disease is most often spread by the bite of rat fleas. However, other animals may also be carriers. Please do not touch anything, since it occasionally is spread by contact. In addition, wash your hands thoroughly with soap and water followed by an alcohol rinse. Make certain to soak your clothes in boiling water."

Maurice then turned to Sherlock Holmes and said, "Sherlock, I don't understand why you are involved in this. The death is clearly due to animal contact. I wouldn't think this is your cup of tea."

I couldn't get over the fact concerning the familial resemblance of Sherlock Holmes and Maurice Verner. They were very tall, strong but wiry, and had hawk-like noses and peering gray eyes.

Sherlock Holmes directed his sharp features toward his cousin and proclaimed, in his piercing tenor voice, "Maurice, one death due to plague would not be particularly disturbing, especially after a journey to a forest. However, four such cases would be an epidemic. This is especially true after they all occurred in a luxurious hotel in the middle of the city of London. The authorities are highly disturbed. Mycroft has been alerted, and he has asked me to follow up."

Maurice responded in his more mellifluous baritone, the tone that suited his female admirers, "But even four could indicate a locus of infection which can be eradicated. They could have wandered into a park with infected squirrels, for example."

"None of them had left the hotel for several days. They have been at a business conference. None of the four infections took place in adjoining hotel rooms, and no sick animals have been noted," continued Sherlock Holmes.

Maurice looked up quickly and exclaimed, "This is another matter! We need to investigate and put a stop to it! Clearly more cases will be expected. There will be panic and the hotel would have to close its doors."

Sherlock Holmes continued, "I have already discussed the issue with the management of the Langdon Hotel, where these deaths occurred. The staff and doctor on call have been told to notify me if they have any guest who has the following symptoms: Chills, malaise, high fever above 102°, muscle cramps, seizures, and of course, swollen lymph glands. Unfortunately, most of these signs are common symptoms, so I have asked Doctor Watson to review the reports and travel to the hotel to evaluate the potential patients. Maurice, I would like you to join us at the hotel to examine the rooms involved. The latest one has been left untouched for our examination. Are you interested?"

Maurice, now enthusiastic, smiled and replied, "I will be very pleased to lend a hand."

He then scribbled a note on a prescription pad and called down, "Billy, make sure this note gets to my interns at Bart's! First, get us a coach for our trip to the Langdon Hotel. Tell my residents that they may find me there after they have finished processing this corpse."

Covering the body with a clean sheet, looking towards us he stated, "My associates, who are studying for their doctorates, will be perfectly capable of continuing the analysis of the specimens. This would be an excellent topic for their theses. The fact that this is part of an epidemic need not be mentioned."

On the way out he looked in at Jeannine, his wife, and her apprentice, Janice, who were stitching their samples of fabric art. Maurice informed them of his impending absence saying, "I might miss lunch, but I hope to join you for tea."

Jeannine tossed her blonde hair and rewarded her husband's consideration with a loving dimpled smile.

She then said, "Please don't forget that we have a dinner engagement at the residence of Lord and Lady Clemmons. Remember, they are talking about using my design services to decorate their new home."

"Yes, dear," Maurice replied. "I will home by five P.M. to dress for our engagement. Lord Clemmons has mentioned a possible donation to my new bacteriology suite at Bart's. I had better be nice to him."

Before taking his leave, Maurice leaned into the sewing room to give Jeannine a husbandly kiss on the cheek. Then, the three of us descended to our mud room, donned our rain apparel and hats, and quickly ran out to the waiting enclosed coach.

The ride to the Langdon was without note. Sherlock Holmes, ever willing to be educated on a topic upon which he was working, quizzed me about the disease of bubonic plague, its history, and origin.

When we arrived, there were two additional interns who studied with Maurice. Apparently, they were not appropriately dressed to enter the confines of the establishment. The staff of elegant hotels looked askance at young men wearing hospital attire. However, a word from Sherlock Holmes provided all of us passage into this lofty hotel, and we commenced to walk up to the fifth level, the floor upon which the targeted rooms were located. Room 507 was guarded by two constables. As soon as they recognized Sherlock Holmes, we were allowed to pass therein.

On the bed was a rumpled sheet covered with sticky dark pus. Maurice instructed his apprentices to roll up the bed clothes into a sheet and transmit them to his laboratory. He then instructed them to journey to the morgue to perform a necropsy and bacteriological examination of the four victims of this disease.

As they left, Sherlock Holmes whipped out his huge glass and began crawling on his knees, examining the floor of the room. Having learned that the other rooms had been thoroughly cleansed, he shook his head and declared, "That was a big mistake. I hope that the servants were not subjected to the disease. It is a shame that their welfare is often overlooked. Maurice, please have your associates gather the house staff, and examine each member for disease. And have them get a recent medical history. Then, please meet us in the back hall to help us investigate further."

Sherlock Holmes inserted several specimens that he had lifted from the carpet into envelopes and put them into a sack that he always carried.

He said, "We can examine these items in detail in Maurice's laboratory. Meanwhile, we will explore an area in the hotel that is never encountered by the high-paying guests."

With that, he beckoned us to follow him through a door at the end of the hall. I had never seen the inner workings of a hotel before, and I received an education. There was a huge, smelly room. There were baskets loaded with soiled bedding waiting to be laundered. There were brooms and mops piled in the corners and piles of damp rags. But what caught Holmes' attention was a table of shoes. Each pair had a square of paper that seemed to be a room identification. Next to the shoes were containers of shoe wax, brushes, and polishing cloths.

Holmes smiled and said,

"I think I know how the infection was deposited into the rooms. "

Maurice stopped and picked up one of the shoes. Using a forceps, he withdrew an insect. It was moving back and forth on the end of the pincers.

"Sherlock, please loan me your magnifying lens," Maurice requested of Holmes.

After a quick examination Maurice exclaimed, "As I anticipated, the insect is a rat flea. Gentlemen, take a look at it."

After we examined Maurice's trophy, he collected a few more such specimens.

Following that respite, Holmes continued his search around the periphery, with us at his heels. He smiled again and said, "I think I have it. The evidence produced by Maurice was the final clue."

He pointed at several circular holes in doors in the walls. They indicated the entrance to closets. When he opened a closet door, our noses were assaulted by a blast of fetid odor. The smell eclipsed any that I had encountered in the field of battle or the military hospital. The entrance of one revealed a pile of lifeless bodies of decaying cats and young white rats. A small hole in the exterior wall allowed a waft of air to carry the smell of mortifying flesh into the room.

He exclaimed, "What a nefarious scheme. Whoever carried out this crime was very clever and devious."

Using a pair of forceps, Holmes showed us the contents of his sample envelopes. From one, he retrieved what I recognized as the feces of rats. From the next, he demonstrated the white fur of laboratory rats, and the last contained the spoor of cats.

"Now I know how the crime was perpetrated. Subsequently, we will need to determine why it was done, who the victims were, and who was the perpetrator."

I replied, feeling as dense as usual, "Holmes, please explain to me what you mean."

"Elementary, my friend," he replied. "Every night the lodgers' servants put out their masters' shoes to be polished. Every morning they are returned, brightly shined by the hotel staff, who is hoping for a nice remuneration for their service. Apparently, this room is the work room. The person who picks up the shoes inserted infected young rats, infested with rat fleas, into them. When the men's servants are scurrying to collect their masters' shoes, they are too harried with activities to note the contents. In the darkened rooms, the rats scuttle out unseen and quickly find their way into the hall, seeking food and escape. The fleas remain behind to pass infestation to the resident. Eventually, the rats are captured by the cats who are allowed to patrol the back hall to eradicate vermin. The felines sequester their prey in their home base in the closet. The young laboratory rats were selected because they fit easily into the toe areas of the shoes and can be hidden in the recesses. Being cultivated artificially, they have never learned to survive on their own, and will quickly perish. The cats, no doubt, died from the infection. However, we still have a lot of detection to do. Now that the hotel staff can prevent further infection, it is up to us to stop further such activities at the source. There is no doubt that the evil villain has a serious reason to go through as much effort as he did. I'm certain that he will try again in another clever manner. Where did the infection come from, who wanted to generate these infections and why, and how do we bring the miscreant to justice? We must get to the bottom of this. Perhaps Maurice will have some information to add."

Holmes and I had agreed to return to Baker Street to retrieve our mail while Maurice would stop off at the morgue to communicate with members of his staff who were assisting the medical examiner and police to review the contents of the pockets of the men who had died from the plague. We planned to meet for tea at Maurice's facility, the one that I had vacated after rejoining Holmes.

Sherlock and I arrived at Maurice's medical facility at just after 4:45 in the afternoon. The group had gathered in his laboratory. Jeannine was showing Maurice drawings of the pictures of the lesions from the infected man. Janice was supplying sketches of the microscopic field from slides. As we entered, Maurice welcomed us with a smile stating, "My female companions and students are making great progress towards a book on infectious disease. While they were working here, my two medical colleagues visited the morgue for additional information. All of the bodies of the first three victims had been removed and buried to avoid the spread of the plague. All four men had been identified by the calling cards in their pockets. The names of the three are John MacCormick, James MacDougall, and Sylvester Campbell. The one on my examining table is Hamish Macalester. According to their identifications, they all represent a development company named 'Highland Homes LTD' in the town of Viking-Corner Village on Lewis Island in the northwest corner of Scotland. According to the map, it is located in the northwest coast of Scotland on a small outlet to 'The Minch.' There is no direct train to the village, so if we need to go there, we will have to go by ship from the mainland. We can travel by express train to Glasgow and then up the west coast on a local. To cross over, we can take a ferry. We can voyage around the island on the water."

Sherlock Holmes looked at me and asked, "Have you ever been to that area?"

I answered, "I'm sorry, I never got that far afield. I'm from Edinburgh. That's where I took my basic medical training. Then, desiring an advanced medical degree and wanting the adventure of living in London, I received my doctoral validation at the University of London Medical after further training at Bart's. I do know, however, that the area in that section of my homeland is rough and burly. There are tales asserting that even the Vikings were afraid to venture into that area. There are stories of a high tower surrounded by a high wall and a moat in Viking-Corner Village. Somehow, when the Viking pillagers dared to approach the area, their low-sided boat was swamped with a wall of water. I think that early English explorers who attempted to determine the veracity of the stories were met with opposition by the very unfriendly residents of the area."

The ever-prepared Maurice unfolded a map of Northwestern Scotland on the floor. We crouched down and identified a shipping line that had passenger traffic from Glasgow to the villages along the coast.

He looked up and said, "I will book passage for us on a first class coach to Glasgow. From there, we can get a special steam launch to our destination, avoiding the stop-and-go railroad trip, and giving us more flexibility to explore when we get there. Are you gentlemen available to leave Wednesday morning from the Baker Street Station?"

"Yes," Holmes replied, after I nodded my assent. "We can meet for breakfast at six in the morning for the eight o'clock train and discuss further plans, if necessary. I suggest that we come armed with revolvers and cudgels. Hopefully we will find an inn to put up in, and to gather local gossip."

After a very nice tea, Holmes and I returned to our Baker Street rooms for a rest, reading of the mail, and glance at the newspapers. As prearranged, Maurice met us Tuesday morning for breakfast. He said, "I have located the logical purveyor of the laboratory rats. We can find out who purchased the animals. As you know, the experimental use of animals is not looked upon with much favor in England. Places that deal in such animals do not advertise to the public. I acquire mine from Bart's. They try to keep the source of their stock secret, but I have an informant at the hospital. Are you ready to accompany me to that vendor?"

Holmes asked, "Is that the only one?"

"Yes," Maurice responded," I asked several sources at Bart's and at other research facilities that my Bart's colleague suggested. None other came to mind. If that one doesn't work out, we will have to try further."

After a hearty breakfast of bacon, eggs, toast and marmalade, and curried rice, we sent Billy out to acquire a coach. Using the satisfactory closed wagon that provided warm and dry passage, we took the long ride to a very undesirable section of London near the Woking docks. There were no signs on the two-story shack towards which we followed Maurice. Maurice knocked loudly on the ramshackle door. A face appeared in the window and the passage was rapidly swung open. Maurice recognized him right away.

He whispered, "The man's name is Granger. He used to work in the hospital laboratory. It appears that he has gone into business on his own."

The chubby, gray haired middle-aged man in a stained coat and tails said, "Dr. Verner. Please come in. Do you need any animals? Usually I see you at Bart's, but I would be happy to satisfy your experimental needs. However, I'm surprised to see you at my doorstep."

Maurice led our way quickly into a large room lined with cages of varied sorts. The low level of mixed fecal odors assaulted my nostrils, but I was happy to note that the facility was sparkling clean, as were the cages. The cleansing had somewhat diminished the expected smell, considering the large animal stock in a closed rom. The smell of pine tar indicated the seriousness that the owner honored in his desire to supply well cared for specimens.

Maurice smiled and said, "Mr. Granger, my inspection indicates that you take very good care of your animals. I'm planning a very large project, and I would like to get a reference from you so that I could get their opinion. I'm particularly interested in male baby rats. I'm doing a study on the effect of coal tar on their growth rate."

"I have just the man to give you a review of my rat stock. Unfortunately, I just ran out. But I can have more in a month." Granger replied.

"Well, to get started I only need ten animals. Maybe I can get a few from your latest buyer. Let me order 100 for future delivery. Here is an advance payment of fifty pounds. I hope that is sufficient"

Smiling broadly, Granger responded, "Thank you for the order. I will contact my supplier right away. Here is the latest buyer's name and home address. I know where to contact you."

And then Mr. Granger scribbled a name and address on a slip of paper.

Shaking hands with Mr. Granger, Maurice said, "Thank you for your future supply of rats. Do you know where I can contact your customer locally?"

Granger replied, "I'm sorry. I think that he has returned home. He said that his experiments had been completed. You will need to write to him at his house to get a review and obtain the rats. He can send them to you by water."

Maurice replied, "Thank you very much. Please contact me when my order has arrived."

As we left, we turned the corner and standing under the sun light read the name and address of the person who had acquired the young rats. We were surprised to read:

> Sir Josiah Macalester
> Gaelic Estates
> Viking-Corner Village
> Lewis Island

Sherlock Holmes noted, "Watson, isn't the name on the card the same last name as one of the dead men, the one we were examining? I think that his first name was Hamish, the same as your middle name, if I recall correctly."

"Yes it is," I replied. "I wouldn't be surprised if the person who acquired the rats used in the murders was related to one of the victims."

"Well, that might be a tentative hypothesis. But we need more facts. It looks as if our planned voyage to Lewis Island will be required." replied Holmes.

When Holmes and I returned to Baker Street, Holmes explored his files and found a listing for Sir Josiah Macalester. Holmes declared, "He is a Baronet from a long line of Scottish warriors. Unfortunately for him, the family's fortunes have taken a negative turn, and the estate is close to bankruptcy. At first I thought it might be a family feud that caused this problem. Now it appears that filthy lucre may be at fault. However, since 'Norwood," I have become more careful in reaching solutions."

Then we had a surprise visitor. Unexpectedly, Maurice arrived at our door with his fellow government agent Mr. Melas.

After a round of friendly greetings, Maurice said, "From Mr. Macalester's belongings, I have obtained the agenda of the business conference that the four murdered men attended. Also, there were his hand-written notes. To sum it up, three of Mr. Macalester's business partners wanted to sell his estate and use the money for commercial development on Lewis Island. It appears that they had a heated discussion. Mr. Macalester resisted this commercial development and, along with his brother, the Baronet, claimed that he wanted to retain their proud family holdings. However, the three other men had already loaned the brothers large amounts of money and wanted to recoup their losses. I can understand, although not condone, the reason for the deaths of the three dissenters. But who would have killed the Baronet's brother? I suppose that he would have been allied with his brother. Could this be an evil plan that went wrong in the hands of inexperienced villains?"

Then Melas took his turn to speak. "I have another piece of information. As you know, I have contacts within the government's secret intelligence agency."

Pulling a rolled sheet of paper out of his pocket, he carefully laid it open on Holmes' deal topped table. On it was pictured Mr. Macalester, with his name on the top, stating 'Wanted Dead or Alive for Murder on Lewis Island.' The reward was 100 pounds sterling.

"Note this wanted poster for Hamish Macalester." said Melas. He clearly has a history of murder. And I have a warrant for his arrest. I trust that you will permit me to accompany you to Lewis Island since that is the address on his brother's card. Perhaps we can get to the bottom of this mystery."

On the appointed day, Mr. Melas picked us up in a government coach bearing the crown's medallions. It was pulled by two stalwart stallions. We drove quickly through the early morning darkness to be deposited at Baker Street Station, the initial point of our long journey to Lewis Island. Slowly we wandered to the coffee shop for breakfast. The pounding of the locomotives was replaced by the tinny clatter of metal utensils and ceramic vessels. The hot steam and burning coal were shut out as we entered the door to the fragrant odor of freshly brewed coffee.

Melas addressed us, as we munched on our breakfast confections, "Don't be surprised if we are accosted in the railway station before we even leave for Scotland. Our adversary is very clever and may wish to remove us from our investigation. He may be aware that we are tracking him. If he is not here, we can still continue our trip."

However, as we left the café and the entrance of a darkened alley, we were approached by two figures coming into view. Our attention was accosted by a familiar voice and the squeaking of a young animal. A recognized voice said, "Turn down this passage."

It was the purveyor of animals, who had been so helpful days before. As we came under a street lamp we could verify this fact. Accompanying him was a man who appeared identical to the deceased Hamish Macalester. Both men were holding young rats and appeared prepared to throw them on us.

Maurice asked, "Why have you done this? We are only trying to catch the murderer of your brother. I assume that you are Sir Josiah Macalester. I thought that you would welcome our assistance."

A clearly Scottish brogue chuckled and said, "You think that you are so smart. You will die for your impertinence."

As they threw the animals at us, our cricket training paid off. We caught the animals in our well-gloved hands and tossed them into the sacks that we had previously placed into our pockets.

The well-known voices of Mr. Lestrade and a colleague of his both said, "We bagged our dangerous criminals. We will soon have them securely cuffed and jailed."

The next speaker was Maurice. He said, "This plan of ours went off without a hitch."

I responded, "I think that you could have prepared us for this action. Maybe we could have had our weapons out."

Maurice countered, "The villains are not trained killers. I expected them to try to kill us in the only way that they knew how to. And as non-professionals, they would never have been alert to your following them. We needed to catch them in the act. We have no other evidence, since they killed any possible witnesses by the use of the plague bacillus."

Sherlock Holmes then spoke, "I admire your plan, although it did take some risk and bravado. The only way it would work would be for us to be gloved and on our guard. But how did you know what they would do?"

Maurice responded, "I reasoned that no one would kill his brother without a good reason. First of all, when I saw the wanted poster, I realized that the dead man was not Hamish Macalester. Fortunately, Jeannine had drawn a sketch of the victim. The dark facial blemish is not on the poster. If that mark had existed on the wanted person, it would have been clearly indicated on the sign, to assist in identification. I suggest the following scenario. The man in the morgue was actually the Baronet, Hamish's brother. With his death reported, the authorities would cease looking for him. Hamish, posing as Sir Josiah, and his colleague, who was familiar with animal diseases, decided to kill all of the claimants to the money from the sale of the estate. He was so greedy that he even killed his brother, who wanted to retain it.

We waved goodbye, as Inspector Lestrade and his constable dragged the two evil men off to the lock-up. Our telegram from the train station informed Mycroft Holmes that the threat of a plague epidemic had been thwarted. We, on the other hand, navigated by foot to the pub next to the station for a well earned pint of stout. As is often the case, our attention was now turned to more general matters. We soon lost interest after the successful conclusion of a case.

My only regret is that we could not continue our journey to Scotland, my place of birth and upbringing. I have never been to the area in question. I understand Glasgow and Lewis Island are both very interesting. I will need to plan a trip to that area as soon as I refill my bank account.

The Adventure of the Poison Tea Epidemic

We were residing at the time in furnished lodgings close to a library where Sherlock Holmes was pursuing some laborious researches in Early English **charters** - researches which led to results so striking that they may be the subject of one of my future narratives.(The Adventure of the Three Students, April 1895)

After the adventure that took place at the onset of the Great War in August 1914, during a quiet time over Scotch and soda, my friend Sherlock Holmes finally gave me the permission to publish the event that brought us to one of England's great universities in a search for clues to another mystery – The Adventure of the Tea Epidemic. The name of the university and its locale must still be concealed due to the fact that some of the principals in the story, published as the 'Adventure of the Three Students,' are still alive, though elderly. I pray that my readers will forgive my occasional use of spellings and references more appropriate to an American, but my language has been contaminated by my three-year sojourn in Baltimore, Maryland obtaining a fellowship in neurological diseases at Johns Hopkins University School of Medicine.

If I recall, the story that I will name 'The Adventure of the Poison Tea Epidemic' began in the early spring of 1895. March had been particularly cold and dry that year, and we were welcoming the anticipated sunshine and warmth of April, only to experience a week of torrential rains. Being alone after the sad occasion of the death of my dear Mary, I had retaken residence in my old home on Baker Street with Mr. Sherlock Holmes. Since most doctors were unavailable after surgery hours, I was often called upon during those times to render emergency medical service. In addition, I was serving two shifts in the neuroscience facility at St. Bart's to keep my hand in and to provide additional income for entertainment.

I had been sitting in my favorite chair by the window, although the heavy downpour impeded the light to some extent. I had just finished *Lancet*, the *British Medical Journal*, and several treatises on experimental neurosurgery, when I noticed that Holmes had installed his large capacity curved briar into his mouth. This signaled the need to organize his papers that were strewn into every corner of our sitting room, into his notebooks and files. Unimpeded, after a few hours work, he would have our quarters as neat as a pin. Since this was much to my liking, I thought it best to sneak off of the premises. Otherwise, seeing my presence, he might feel impelled to narrate one of his old adventures instead of completing the organizational task. I glanced at the huge grandfather clock that had been a gift from the King of Scandinavia, and noted that it was past 3 P.M.

I quietly tip-toed to the door and was approaching the stairs, when glancing back, I saw Holmes remove his pipe after taking a large inhalation. He said, "Have a nice evening." He smiled briefly, as was his custom, and returned to his chores.

As I entered the street, I noticed that the rain had temporarily ceased and the sky was finally clearing. I encountered a messenger and gave him a note to deliver to my old friend Thurston, stating, "Thurston, old man, are you up to a nice dinner at our club, a few drinks, and several rounds of billiards. If so meet me at our club. I will be there in less than 30 minutes."

After that, I beckoned a Hansom cab over, and went on a short, splashy ride to my club. I climbed the flight of stairs, entered the reading room, and ordered a Scotch and soda to while away the time and read the *Guardian*.

After only a brief interlude, I spotted Thurston wiping his feet at the entrance to the chamber, his hat still dripping from the renewed downpour. After the servant had removed his rain gear, I noticed that my friend was still thin and well built. He looked as if he could still command his platoon as he had done in Afghanistan, His smile revealed bright teeth over his red mustache that was spotted with specks of gray. I ordered a Scotch and soda for him, and he sat next to me.

Picking up the drink from the intervening table, after we shook hands and seated ourselves, he took a sip and said, "Just the thing after a hard day of filing taxes for the lords and ladies of the kingdom. I'm happy to see you for a long savored relaxation." He continued in his deep baritone voice, just slightly showing the deleterious effects of age on its timbre, "I hope that you are ready for a serious match. I haven't played in two weeks, and I'm anxious to deprive you of some of your money."

After downing our cocktails, we were notified that our table was ready for our dinner of rare prime rib with tasty potatoes and vegetables, and a bottle of Bordeaux. Afterwards, satiated, we went up the one flight of old oaken stairs to the beautiful mahogany paneled billiard room. We were enjoying a leisurely game of three cushion billiards and our second aged cognac when a melee burst out at the entrance to the portal.

Our play was interrupted by one of the servants. He made me aware of the fact that the commissionaire, whom I had known for many years, had invaded the facility. Unlike the usually staid demeanor of the former non-commissioned officer in her Majesty's marines, the commissionaire came bursting into the billiard room. Gone was he usual military bearing and stiff upper lip. Instead, he was trembling all over. His usually stern face was red with grief and his eyes flush with tears.

He exclaimed in a loud voice, "My youngest child Edith is dying from pneumonia. She is burning with fever and can scarcely breathe. She is shaking all over her little body. My doctor expects her to die by morning."

Obviously, it was my ethical duty to comply with this urgent call to service. I scooped up my bag, said a hasty farewell and apology to my opponent and rushed down the stairs following my old commissionaire whom I had known for many years and who had always provided faithful service. I dashed out the door to find a four wheeler peopled by the commissionaire, an old woman and a tiny infant wrapped in woolen blankets. Without a second's delay, I yelled to the cabbie, "Off to St. Bart's as fast as you can go. If you make it in 20 minutes you will earn an extra sovereign."

My stethoscope informed me that the female infant was in the last stages of pneumonia. She was barely breathing and her lungs were congested. Also, I didn't need the assistance of a thermometer to determine that she was highly febrile. I knew there was only one chance for her: the new experimental serum being developed at the Serology Institute in the research area of St. Bart's. The rabbit antiserum containing antibodies to all three strains of diplococccus was her only hope. When we had entered the new facility, I summoned the colleagues with whom I had researched for several years prior to switching to neurology. They quickly arrived, all five of them, from the areas in which they were working. My medical colleagues and I spent all night ministering to the baby with multiple intravenous injections of serum, an ice bath, and aspirin. Finally, at 2:00 in the morning, she reached the expected climax. By God's willing answer to my prayers and the power of the new medication, the fever broke, and she was again spirited and well. Joyfully, I left her and her father in the loving care of the hospital staff. I trudged out into the deep night after promising to return at noon to see how she was faring. Finally, finding a cab, I made my way back to

Baker Street, not recalling how I made it up the stairs and into my bed.

I didn't arise until a quarter past 11 A.M., if you can believe the old grandfather clock that was provided by the King of Scandinavia. I was in desperate need for a cup of hot coffee, and was grateful that the smell of fresh beverage filled the air. However, my ability to obtain this beverage was retarded by my colleague's actions. Now, I may have certain character flaws, but when it comes to plucking out a thick facial hair at the breakfast table, I draw the line. Not only was Sherlock Holmes performing that less-than-elegant act that should have been restricted to the bathroom, but he was using the highly polished coffee pot as his mirror.

"Holmes, if you don't mind, I would like to have the coffee pot. Maybe you could find a mirror in your bedroom for your preening." I said with some asperity.

Holmes turned to me with a smile, handed me the coffee pot, and said, "I see that you made a late night of it. What did you and Thurston do after leaving the club? Did you seek female companionship? I tried to leave a message for you, but my courier could only say that you rushed out."

"Holmes, what did you want me for? You weren't busy when I left for supper and billiards. I'm busy now. I must eat a quick breakfast and hurry off to St. Bart's. I have a pneumonia patient," I replied.. "When I return, you can tell me why you went to the trouble to summon me."

Holmes replied, "All will be revealed. Here is a sandwich that Mrs. Hudson made for me. Take your coffee with you and eat in the cab."

Grateful to Holmes for the thoughtfulness he occasionally showed when appropriate, I was even more grateful that my miniature patient had now recovered. However, I was shocked the commissionaire had left the facility and the child was being ministered to by previously seen elderly woman.

"Where is Bracket?" I asked loudly, "and who are you?"

Smiling gently as she stroked the child, the gray haired woman said, "Don't fret doctor, I am Edith's aunt Teresa. Mr. Bracket is my brother. He rushed off after seeing another doctor. I don't know why or where."

I rushed out to the nurse's station yelling, "What happened to the commissionaire? What has caused him to leave his daughter who is just now recovering from pneumonia?"

A beautiful young blonde-haired nurse, whom I had often visited for conversation, walked over to me and said, "It's Mr. Bracket's wife and other two children, a boy of 2 and a girl of 5. They seem to be suffering from a severe poisoning. You may find them in the women's ward. Follow me."

I walked behind her, admiring both her figure and her control of the situation. She said, pointing to the left, "Go this way. The doctors are in with them now. Perhaps you would like to take charge of the case, since the men ministering to them are only young interns."

She turned and smiled at me, and then quickly left for her station as I reluctantly watched her go. "Well, another time would be more propitious," I thought.

As I entered the room, I quickly sized up the situation. Bracket was sitting in a chair, his head in his hands. His wife and two children were shaking all over, in an obviously nervous state. The young interns rose to greet me, and then recognizing a senior colleague backed away as if awaiting my orders.

"These people are obviously suffering from a poisoning. Their moans indicate a state of hallucination. It appears to be some type of food poisoning, since there are no wounds on the bodies or bleeding, as I can tell from your notes. You must clear their bodies as quickly as possible. Pump their stomachs, apply enemas, flush with copious amounts of water, and then administer activated charcoal and very strong tea."

"No tea! It's poison!" yelled Mrs. Bracket, as she sat upright in the bed. Then she quickly fell back to her supine position.

I ordered, "Cancel the tea until further notice. Continue with the other instructions."

Observing the patients more closely, I began to recognize their symptoms as I slowly recalled the lectures I had received many years ago. They had undergone seizures, hallucinations, tremors, and now they expressed that they were nauseous. There was no diarrhea that one would expect from typical food poisoning. I hypothesized that they were suffering from a mild case of ergotism. I turned to my youngest colleague, an Indian, and said, "Mr. Singh, please run to the chemists and bring me amyl nitrite solution. Have the woman inhale 0.3 ml. and give the children 0.1 ml."

Turning to the other two men, I said, "Mr. Riley and Mr. Addison, please watch them carefully and keep me abreast of their progress."

As my young colleagues were ministering to my new patients, I went over to the commissionaire. Kneeling next to him, I asked "What is happening? Why are your wife and children ill and you are not? Did you drink any tea? Did it have a strange taste?"

He responded with a tremulous voice, "We were just sitting down to tea when I had to rush Edith off to the hospital. Thus, I had no tea. When I was at Edith's bedside, talking to my sister, a doctor took me away to see my family in this state. They were yelling and convulsing. No one knew what to do."

"Fortunately, I have neurological training and I recognized signs of chemical poisoning. Has anyone eaten freshly baked rye bread or anything unusual?"

He replied, "No sir. We had eaten nothing until tea was served. I left with Edith and told them to continue the tea service while I rushed to find you. Fortunately, I know where you often go when you are not on Baker Street, and I knew that it was not one of your work nights."

I said, "So it would appear that the tea was contaminated with rye bearing the ergot fungus. That is most unusual and surprising. Please stay here and watch your family. I will ask the nurse to bring you Edith on my way out. Now I must summon Mr. Sherlock Holmes. This sounds like a rare mystery that is beyond my power to discern." I said as I turned to leave.

Running out to the busy street, I spotted my friend, the cabbie Jonathon. Handing him 5 shillings, I shouted, "Bring Mr. Sherlock Holmes. Tell him that Bracket's family has been poisoned and such a criminal act requires his immediate attention. Other people may be at risk."

While I awaited Holmes' visit, I noticed that the victims were recovering from their attack. Finally, Mrs. Bracket turned to me and said, "Dr. Watson, thank you very much for saving our lives. We must get that tea out of the house before anyone else gets sick."

I turned to one of my young colleagues and ordered, "Addison, find out where these people live. Scour the house for poisons and bring me any tea that you find."

Addison, the doctor in training, responded yes sir and hurried off. I knew the lad well. As the tall sandy-haired slim figure dashed off, I had an opportunity to question both Mr. and Mrs. Bracket.

Turning to Mrs. Bracket, I asked, "Where did you buy the tea? We must retrieve any that they sold or still have in hand in case there are more poisoned lots. Also, did it taste unusual?"

"Well, doctor, I didn't purchase the tea. It was a gift from one of my husband's employers, John Alexander. It seems that the lady of the house bought the wrong kind of tea, according to her husband. She said that he hadn't bought the tea, but that it was a gift from his employer's neighbor, Sir James Green, who had given it to Mr. Alexander."

"So the tea wasn't originally intended for you. It was originally intended for Mr. Alexander," I stated.

"That is correct, Dr. Watson. But the tea tasted a little like rye bread. I really didn't like it, but you can't look a gift horse in the mouth."

Just then, Holmes rushed in and took over the scene. Holding the paper package of the tea that had just arrived, he turned to the commissionaire and said, "I have a very important job for you. Get as many men as you can and go to the shop that sells this brand of tea, locate all of the recent customers, and bring all you can find to my lodgings on Baker Street. Here are several shillings to get the necessary cooperation. Tell the proprietor that Sherlock Holmes thinks that they are selling poisoned tea."

Relieved that he now had an important assignment, and that his entire family was recovering and in the hands of medical professionals, Bracket resumed his normal erect stature and bearing, and marched out of the room quickly with precise steps.

Holmes and I made the short carriage ride to Bracket's abode to see if we could find any other evidence that would point to a source of poison or, as I thought, ergot contaminated rye. We arrived at the small lodging contained on the third floor of a brown brick building in the working class neighborhood housing the workers who served the local hospital and medical offices. Holmes quickly penetrated the building entrance and the door to the apartment without requiring a key, using methods that he had acquired from his more nefarious colleagues. The only thing out of place were the turned over chairs at the kitchen table, some liquid tea drying on the wooden floor, and tea cups containing the dregs of the teas that had not yet been ingested. Otherwise, there was no evidence of foul play. We scoured the two bedrooms, the bath, sitting room, and kitchen without finding anything suspicious. It was obvious that, as good parents, anything hazardous to children was safely under lock and key. We took the used teacups back with us for further examination. Holmes poured the residue of the tea into small glass containers, and secured the opened carton of tea in a canvas bag that he had brought for that purpose.

As we were exiting, Holmes turned to face me and asked, as a teacher does to a student, "You have examined the contents of this abode. Using your powers of observation and deduction, do you think the Bracket was the kind of man that would purposely poison his wife and children?"

I replied, "Not at all Holmes. His bed was made with military precision. One could bounce a shilling off of it. His children's beds were covered with care and were warmly dressed. Although one wall in his sitting room was decorated with mementos of his military service, the larger bore many images of his family that far exceeded his personal effects. Also, based on my training as a neuroscientist, I would declare that his grief for his toddler's pneumonia and his reaction to his other family members' illness was genuine and palpable. Have I missed anything? Do you agree?"

"Watson," he declared with a smile. "You are coming along nicely. You make an excellent detective's associate. I agree with your analysis and trust the commissionaire completely."

As soon as we had arrived at our lodgings, Holmes quickly got to work. First he smelled the package of tea and invited me to do the same.

"It smells like rye bread," I said. "I never have experienced that odor in tea before."

Then he cleared his chemical apparatus from the deal topped table and installed a high powered microscope on its surface. Using a forceps, he carefully teased a portion of the solid dregs onto a glass slide. Then he applied a thin cover slip. He slowly lowered the objective to the top of the cover slip, and the slowly raised it until he had what he wanted to see in focus. He smiled and said, "I think that your diagnosis was correct. Take a look."

I carefully repeated his actions until the material was brought into sharp focus. It didn't take me long to recall the lessons that I had learned many years ago. There were tea leaves and what could only be stands of rye stipules.

"Holmes, what I find most revealing are fruiting bodies of the ergot fungus *Claviceps purpurea*. I never thought that I would ever need this knowledge." I said, "My physical diagnosis was correct. I'm pleased that I was able to predict the appropriate therapy."

Holmes replied, "Yes, Watson, you are to be congratulated for medical acumen. Tomorrow we will need to visit the purveyors of this tea for a conversation. I'm certain that they have closed their facility for the night, but we will visit them early in the morning. Meanwhile, you must tell your assistants not to alert the police. If they want to publish this account in a house medical proceedings and report it in Grand Rounds, where it will disappear from public sight but serve to further their careers that would be fine."

I responded, "Why not bring in the police. They can help us gather evidence."

Holmes retorted, "If my supposition is correct, Bracket will benefit financially from my solution to the crime. If the perpetrators are jailed, which may be unlikely unless we can find more direct evidence tying them to the actual crime, no one will benefit from the misfortunes suffered by his wife and children."

Having accomplished all that we could, Holmes and I returned to our lodgings for our own high tea, being careful to inspect the label, sniff the contents, and to settle down for a rest. I was pleased by our conversation and in a relaxed frame of mind during the entire evening. As we sat, I asked Holmes why we didn't go to the tea merchant ourselves to get the information. He replied, "Everyone likes Commissionaire Bracket. They all use his services and trust him. Had we shown up, we might have encountered suspicion and resistance. Also, I think that I would like to light a pipe and cogitate upon the issues. Why would someone give John Alexander poisoned tea. Or if we are to believe his wife, why would someone give it to Sir James, or if we want to take it a step further, was the commissionaire's family the ultimate target? Then, is there a large supply of poisoned tea in the market? I'm certain that Bracket and his cohorts will round up all of the supplies. Then, we will need to scour the papers that I asked Billy to pick up for us as we enjoyed our tea and crumpets. And finally, why did the tea have a rye taste? I have a monograph on 226 blends of tea including the appearance of cooked and raw leaves, and a description of each flavor. I have never encountered a tea that is flavored with rye, and I can't see why anyone would want it. Tomorrow, we will have accumulated enough data to guarantee a meaningful conversation."

Holmes' last act for the evening was to send our buttons out to acquire copies of all of the newspapers before he allowed the lad to leave for the evening.

I awoke at my usual late hour to find Holmes deeply studying the newspapers that were piled up next to his ham and eggs and coffee mug. He had a glint in his deep gray eyes and a devilish smile in his face that predicted a bad ending to the perpetrators of this mischief. I quickly ingested my breakfast and left for my morning shift at St. Bart's. Also, I needed to see to my four patients and handle any financial issues. Sherlock Holmes guaranteed that he would add this expense to whoever would end up paying for his investigative services.

As I left, Holmes said, "Are you up to a trip in the area of my former university? I need to do a search of ancient British charters and you might enjoy the environs. We leave this afternoon from Baker Street Station."

I replied, "I will be packed quickly, a skill I learned in the army medical service." Then I rushed down to the street to get the cab that our buttons had reserved for me.

I arrived on time at St. Bart's and met with my staff. I congratulated my students for a job well done and warned them about avoiding publicity. I brought a sample of the tea dregs for them to evaluate as background for their report but told them that the source of the materials is still under investigation and cannot be revealed. Then, with my interns in tow, I examined my patients, saw that they were now recovered from their travails, and released them from their involuntary hospital confinement. I informed Bracket and his wife that the poisoning incident must be kept secret so that Mr. Holmes is able to adjudicate the issue and obtain remuneration for them.

After two hours of patient rounds, I bid farewell to my staff, wished them a good day, and returned to my Baker Street lodgings for a well-deserved lunch and nap. However, the nap was not to be. As I arrived, my nose was overwhelmed by the strong odor of tea that masked the pungent smell of his vile pipe tobacco. Holmes' chemical table bore five opened cartons of Paladinium Tea, the same brand that was the source of the ergot poisoning the previous day. The entire surface of his work table was covered with microscope slides and cover slips.

Holmes said, "Ah Watson, you are just in time for our next pieces of evidence. All five cartons of tea that were recently delivered are free of rye particles and fungal spores. Only the box delivered to Sir James Green, who had later given it to Mr. Alexander, was so contaminated. It was not a random event. So, the source of the poisoned tea goes at least as far back as Sir James Green. Although it's possible that the servants despoiled the samples, I suggest that that is not the case. I sent buttons to question Mrs. Bracket, and she said that the box did not look as if it had been opened, or if it had been, it was very well done.

Then he showed me the papers. In the interior pages of the *Guardian*, in the section devoted to agriculture, there was a brief account of cattle poisoning in a rye field near his famous university.

He cried out, "Quick, eat your lunch! A cab awaits our voyage of discovery."

And off we went on a journey that I found out would take us to the city where resides one of England's great universities, and former scholastic residence of Sherlock Holmes before he left to complete his degree at London University and St. Bart's.

As we dashed onto the train and entered the last available first class smoking carriage, I asked Holmes, "Where are we going? What is the purpose of this journey?"

He replied, "We are traveling to the area where I first encountered my university training. Therein is a library replete with official land charters, and a nearby field in which some poor cattle died from eating rye contaminated with the fungus of ergotism. These documents, and ownership of the land may provide further information on the motive for the ergot poisoning that we discovered by accident, and the possible source of the deleterious material."

I immediately understood his objective, but I couldn't understand how this data would apply to a criminal event in far off London. As usual, I was forced to stay on the sidelines, exploring the buildings and town of a university that was foreign to me, while my friend spent hours on the diligent search through dry records that may date back to the formation of the English nation itself. My perambulations and isolation, except for mealtimes, was only interrupted by the brief adventure concerning the copying of the Greek scholarship exam. After only two more days, Sherlock Holmes grabbed me off of the street. In his right hand he held a plethora of documents that were rolled in a bright blue ribbon.

"Come Watson, we must pack our belongings. I now have the solution to the mystery of the devious ergotism event!" he cried. "We must return to London before the trail turns cold!"

We ran for the train just as the whistle was blowing and the conductor yelled, "All aboard."

We hurried into a first class smoker and settled down for the long journey to Baker Street. Holmes busied himself with several newspapers that he had acquired from Professor Soames, and then began studying the documents that had been carried under his long, thin arms.

Knowing that my companion would not permit any conversation as he studied the papers in his hands, I sought out the dining car, had two glasses of dry white wine, and fell into a stupor. The gentle monotonous chug of the locomotive and the delightful view out of the window, after I had returned to my carriage, must have lulled me to sleep. I felt a gentle tap on my shoulder as the conductor cried out, "Baker Street station. All off!"

I noticed that Holmes had now unfolded all of the documents and tied them into a neat pile. The newspapers were shoved under his seat. The edges revealed that several pages had been sampled with a pair of scissors. A smile on Holmes face indicated that someone was not going to be happy in a day or two. The look of concentration thwarted my attempts to converse with him, and I quietly followed him to a Hansom cab and our final ride to our quarters.

After we strode up the 17 steps to our suite, Holmes immediately went to his desk and began writing telegrams. I noted that he was withdrawing his special expensive formal stationery and writing notes with his neat hand. He then called out, "Billy, drop these telegrams at the post office and pay for a reply to each. Then take a cab and hand deliver these to the addresses on the linen envelopes."

With that, Holmes looked at me and said, "Watson, as you see I have been very busy. Please forgive me for ignoring you, but time was of the essence. Please get together your best set of city clothes. We will be entertaining tomorrow at high tea at 5 P.M. at the Paladinium Tea Room in their special tasting room. I expect that we will make the acquaintance of two leaders of our society who, unbeknownst to our friends, have some dark dealings in their past."

"Should I call Gregson or Lestrade?" I asked.

"No Watson, I think that justice will be served better without the intervention of the constabulary. Just be prepared to leave tomorrow at 4:40 P.M."

Then, opening his violin case, he continued; "Now it is time for sweetness and light. Please fix each of us Scotch and soda while I supply some music before we order our supper from Mrs. Hudson."

The following day, I arose a trifle late, even for me, full of a desire to question Holmes about our coming adventure, but alas, he had already stepped out. I was required to fill the day as best I could, walking to Marble Arch and listening to the orators, and then returning for a solitary lunch of fish and chips, and a bitter ale.

Holmes arrived at 4 P.M. already attired in his conservative business dress. He glanced at my selection of dark frock coat, silk tie, and grey striped pants. He nodded in affirmation of my attire. We each picked up our most ornate walking sticks, walked down to the street, and retrieved a four wheeler that our servant had secured for us.

Holmes winked at me and said, "We will make a stop along the way."

Then, we stopped at the residence of Bracket, who was now very elegantly attired in his military dress uniform. Our threesome pulled up at the chic entry to the most expensive tea room in the West End. A liveried footman emerged, opened our carriage door, and guided us past the little old ladies who populated the front room of the shop. We then were escorted up the stairs to the palatial rooms reserved for the special guests. The fashionable décor indicated that we appropriately dressed for the surroundings. The tables were set with glistening silver spoons and stylish imported tea cups and saucers with matching pitchers and lemon service. The walls were adorned with masterworks of art, among which were several oil paintings by Mr. Holmes' great uncle M. Vernet.

The heralded proprietor of the Paladinium Tea Room, Mr. Brooks, was garbed in afternoon formal attire. He greeted each of us individually as an honored guest. His thin mustache accented a very narrow nose on a slight well shaven face that matched his slim build and tiny feet. He carried himself with the grace expected of a doyen of such a fine establishment.

When he approached Sherlock Holmes and shook his hand, he said, "Mr. Holmes, I have always wanted to meet you. I have been following your exploits closely."

Turning in my direction, he extended his hand and gave me a firm shake. "Doctor Watson, I'm extremely pleased to meet the famous author and biographer of Mr. Holmes."

He also greeted the Commissionaire with the respect usually afforded an aristocrat, shaking his hand and thanking him for his courage and service to our queen. He then motioned to a tray of small glasses and invited us to join him in a sherry as we awaited our other visitors.

The two additional men arrived about five minutes later, separately, and each was accompanied by his man servant. After the valets removed the top hats and light overcoats of our visitors, they took away the walking sticks and went down the stairs to the servants' area. Sir James Green and Mr. Horatio Alexander were men of a type who could be considered aristocrats and men of affairs. In many ways they resembled Holmes' former school mate Musgrave. Their attire was in the latest fashion from the best tailors. Their shoes were glistening in the light of the tea room. They were both very pale of skin, and had fair hair. They held their noses up as if to avoid any foul odors and their faces bore the obvious signs of disdain. As they approached the earlier residents of the room, they bowed formally as a sign of recognition. However, they did not offer their hands. They especially looked askance at the uniformed military figure of Commissionaire Bracket who gave each a military salute.

The man identified as Sir James Green said, "Mr. Brooks, I thought that this was to be a private showing. What are the other men doing here?"

Brooks responded as courteously and as well as he could under the circumstances saying, "I thought that you would enjoy the company of other noted gentlemen at this event."

Mr. Alexander said, "Let's get this over with. As long as we are here, I can stand the company of Sir James Green for this short time. Next time, please make certain that you meet us separately. The other men are welcome to join us."

With that, Mr. Brooks clapped his hands and a waiter appeared pushing in a large carboy sloshing hot water. The men were invited to take seats of their choice, and were each provided with a dollop of tea in a strainer. He then poured hot water through each.

Immediately, Sir James burst out, "Are you trying to kill us? This tea is poisoned!"

Shocked by this outburst, the other men pushed their chairs back. Sherlock Holmes asked, "How do you know this tea is poisoned? Is it the smell of rye?"

Sir James shouted, "Are you accusing me of something?"

"No," retorted Sherlock Holmes, "You are accusing yourself." And with that, Holmes finished preparing his cup of tea and began to drink. "Is it the smell of rye? I thought that this was a very pleasant taste."

At Holmes' signal, Bracket and I also drank our tea. Seeing that there was no danger, Mr. Alexander also consumed his tea. Chagrined by this, Sir James followed suit, but with some degree of trepidation.

"What is this about?" asked Sir James angrily. "You tricked me!"

"You tricked yourself," replied Holmes. "Now please seat yourself. I have a story to tell you."

Sir James stood up and attempted to leave. "I have no interest in your tales, you busybody. I'm leaving."

"We three will hold you in here until we have concluded the business of the evening. Mr. Brooks, I think that the Scotch and soda that I brought would be better suited to what follows. Thank you very much for your courtesy. Please sit and listen, since what follows many also be of interest to you."

Mr. Alexander said, "Yes, stay. I want to know what this is about."

After each man had been supplied with their alcoholic beverage, Sherlock Holmes began his recitation. "I received a desperate call from Dr. Watson that Sergeant Major Bracket's wife and children were stricken with ergot poisoning. Now, Dr. Watson is an expert in nervous system disorders. He was able to save the lives of the three individuals, all of whom had ingested tea smelling of rye.

Neither Mr. Bracket nor his daughter was affected because they went to the hospital before they could drink any tea, due to an attack of pneumonia suffered by the child. When Dr. Watson and I inspected Mr. Bracket's domicile, we noted a strong smell of rye. Subsequently, we examined the tea dregs in my laboratory and saw, in the microscope, fragments of rye wheat and *Claviceps purpurea* therein."

"What has that to do with me," yelled Sir James. "I don't even know this man or his family."

As he started again to leave, Bracket, Watson, and even Alexander threw him back in his chair saying, "Somehow, I think that tea was meant for me. My cook told me that it was sent over and I refused it, telling her to destroy it."

"You have been after me all of the years as well. But you can't prove that I'm the source of the poisoned tea."

Sherlock Holmes resumed his professorial manner and continued. "According to Mrs. Bracket, she received the tea from Mrs. Alexander who thought that she was doing a kindness. But the tea, which wreaked havoc with the Bracket family, was clearly intended for Mr. Alexander."

"Then where did the ergot in the tea come from?" asked Sir James belligerently.

"Thank you for the entry to my next story. It seems as if land belonging to you is infested with rye wheat contaminated with ergot."

With that, Sherlock Holmes passed around material clipped from the *Guardian* and more detailed accounts of cattle poisoning from the local press in Holmes' university town. Holmes said, "I also visited the area with Dr. Watson, and looked at all of the land holdings in the area. You, Sir James had access to the ergot contaminated rye."

"If you think that is the case, why don't you turn this over to the police?"

"Because, I do not plan to besmirch your name or that of Mr. Alexander in the press. The society pages would have a field day. Also, it would harm the excellent and well hard earned reputation of the Paladinium Tea Room and its proprietor Mr. Brooks. I have another story that you may find interesting as well,." went on Sherlock Holmes.

He continued, "I researched ancient English charters almost to the beginning of our nation from the Norman conquest. There was a brave and ferocious knight who served William the Conqueror. As a reward for his service, the man was first made a baron of the realm and later was awarded the position of Earl. This gentleman had a succession of heirs, each bearing the noble title and serving the kings of England. Unexpectedly, one of the men had twin sons. He died before the land could be officially awarded to the appropriate heir. After that time, descendents of both have quarreled over the ownership of the estates. That man was your ancestor. Your quarrel dates back to that time. You gentlemen are of the same blood, first cousins several generations removed from the great Earl, who is your ancestor. I now have the copies of all of the documents and land grants. I suggest that you join together in a court action and split the properties equitably, and to cease these useless attempts to murder each other."

"That is good news, Mr. Holmes. I had no idea that we were kin. I only knew that we each were told that the entire tract of land was ours to fight over," said Mr. Alexander. "It does not behoove us to fight each other when, in tandem, we can join our forces and reap the harvest that we deserve. James, I forgive your attempt to harm me if you can see it in your heart to do the same for my past actions."

Sir James stood up, held out his hand and said, "Cousin, it is time that we were partners. We are both very clever at affairs and could reap a great harvest. By now, the value of the land itself is far less valuable that our holdings in properties, money, and investments. "

To everyone's surprise, the two cousins shook hands in friendship and said, in unison, "To making our fortunes." Then, they embraced each other and started to leave arm in arm.

Sherlock Holmes ordered, "Just a minute gentleman. I'm satisfied that you have made a friendly alliance, but there is still the matter of Mr. Bracket and his family who were the innocent victims of your rivalry. Mr. Bracket, thank you for your attendance. Now I wish to speak to the cousins in private with only Doctor Watson as a witness. Mr. Brooks, would you please see the Commissionaire to a cab and pay his fare. I will reimburse you soon."

As they left, Mr. Brooks said, "That is the least I could do for saving my reputation."

After they left, Sherlock Holmes took some very formal looking documents from his pocket. He handed a copy to each gentleman saying, "Here are contracts that I have had formatted by my attorney binding you to an agreement to provide financial remuneration to Mr. Bracket's family. Please read them carefully. You may have a solicitor read over them, but I am firm on the requirements. You will collectively provide money to support a suitable home for Mr. Bracket and his family and scholarships to excellent schools and a university education."

Both gentlemen carefully read the short document, nodded their agreements, and quickly signed both copies.

Sherlock Holmes said, "Thank you gentlemen for your cooperation. I'm happy that everyone will benefit by this day's events. I will have my solicitor finalize these contracts for my signature along with Dr. Watson as witnesses."

Both men smiled broadly. "Thank you, Mr. Holmes. You are truly a miracle worker," said Sir James.

"Yes," added Mr. Alexander. "The words of Dr. Watson's narratives ring true. If ever I am troubled with a serious problem, I will contact you. Expect a check for 1000 pounds for your expenses."

"I will add the same amount to that." Said Mr. Alexander as he two aristocrats strolled off arm in arm.

Sherlock Holmes turned to his friend and said, "Now for some great food, wine, and repartee. We have both been invited by brother Mycroft to join him at his club for dinner."

I turned to Holmes and asked, "How does he know about this?"

Holmes replied, "Brother Mycroft seems to always know what is going on, sometimes before it takes place."

Then off we went seeking transportation to the guest dining room at the Diogenes Club.

Dr. Watson and the Case of the Deadly Honey

Two men were quietly seated in their secluded and heavily locked impenetrable warehouse complex that faced the Detroit River. Both were quietly sipping 30-year old single-malt Scotch and smoking hand-rolled cigars from Tampa, Florida.

They bore a striking resemblance to one another, clean shaven and wiry thin with hawk-like profiles. The older man was in his late seventies, but still had the bearing and physical condition of a much younger man. He had the aquiline appearance that characterized his lineage. He turned to his younger companion and said, "Maurice, since the sad death of your lamented father, my brother, and since I have no children of my own, you are now the next eldest representative of the Verner family. Thus, you are now the heir apparent to our family business. This includes all of its secrets."

Maurice Verner nodded in acknowledgement. He looked around admiring the artifacts in the chamber with highly limited access. It was a replica of Sherlock Holmes' sitting room as described in the Sherlockian Canon, down even to the gasogene and Tantalus. He smiled and said, "Uncle Horace, do you remember when, as a child, I thought that it was actually Sherlock Holmes' room brought from Baker Street in London? I will be honored to serve as your understudy."

Uncle Horace Vernet, who still used the French spelling of his surname, replied, "The first lesson that you will need to learn is that it actually is the real Sherlock Holmes' sitting room. It was brought by our family when we emigrated from England. However, that was not his real name. The stories were written by his friend who used the pen name Dr. John H. Watson and trusted Dr. Arthur Conan Doyle for distribution."

"That is most enlightening," replied the hawk-nosed early-middle-aged Maurice. "Who else knows?"

"Only my wife Juliet shares the secret, of course. But you should tell your wife Alisha. We have no secrets from our spouses in our family."

After the men had finished their cigars and drinks, Horace arose and pulled two pairs of white gloves from a drawer in the roll top oak desk.

"Put these on," ordered Uncle Horace. "I have something very special to show you. You will be astonished."

With that, the older man made a long arm and took an ancient tin dispatch box down from the recess behind the roll top. The box was labeled with a red wax crayon such as that which was once used in chemical laboratories. The title in large upper case block letters was 'Memoirs of Dr. John H. Watson May 1891 to April 1894.'

"Wasn't that the time of the Great Hiatus when it was recorded by Dr. Watson that Sherlock Holmes had died at the Reichenbach Falls in the story entitled the 'Final Problem' and then returned in the story 'Empty House'?" queried Maurice Verner.

"Quite true," replied the older man gingerly holding a fragile yellowed paper in his gloved hand, "But look at this document."

"Holding the ancient document carefully in his cottoned fingers, Maurice expostulated "Wow, it says it's a hand-written story by Dr. Watson himself, titled 'The Case of the Deadly Honey.' The ink is very faded and the paper is looking very fragile. Sherlock Holmes was not around during that time. How can that be?" asked the younger man.

"Well, Maurice, Dr. Watson still had a sense of adventure. These are episodes of his activities during that era when Sherlock Holmes was on a grand tour of the world acting as an emissary for the British Government. Since they were not about Sherlock Holmes, he never had them published."

Seeing that Maurice was very nervous about handling these ancient documents, Horace smiled, took the paper back, and said, "I made enhanced photocopies of the documents so that you could read them more easily," handing Maurice a more modern file folder containing a three-ring binder. "The script has been converted to PDF using OCR. Read these at your leisure."

As they left this sacred room that was scarcely ever used, Maurice rushed to his luxurious suite, kissed his wife hello, and immediately began to read the first account.

Dr. Watson's narrative began as follows:
My heart was filled with grief as I sat morosely attempting to absorb a treatise on mental disorders in the *British Medical Journal*. I haven't been able to concentrate since my best and only true friend, Mr. Sherlock Holmes, recently perished at the Reichenbach Falls in Switzerland. Quickly following this grievous development, my beloved wife Mary died from a fatal case of influenza. Thus, I was overwhelmed with mental anguish. My only true contacts had perished. Only the rush of my medical activities and my researches into mental disorders with Dr. Trevelyan had allowed me to fill the days with distractions. However, in the evening, I fell into a depressed mood. But, the thrilling events that would soon follow would snap me out of this dour mood.

It started this way. My living quarters on the third level of my medical establishment in Kensington were otherwise deserted. I could barely hear the brushing sounds of the broom below me as the boy in buttons was sweeping up prior to preparing my surgery for the following day's events. My house maid had long ago retired to her bedroom for the evening.

My new medical partner, Dr. Verner, who shared my practice, was busily working in his bacteriology lab on the fourth level. As the glamour of my association with Sherlock Holmes had attracted many female clients, I needed his younger and more energetic assistance to get me through the day. Also, his interest in the burgeoning field of bacteriology, and his more recently acquired knowledge that he had obtained during his stay at St. Bart's, was an excellent accompaniment to my expertise in the surgical manipulation of wounds. I was surprised that such an accomplished expert had taken an interest in being my partner.

The quiet was rudely broken by a startling turn of events. My living quarters were harshly invaded by a cacophony of sound that alerted every fiber in my nervous system to the training that I had received on the battlefield. Having jumped to my feet, I reached for my sidearm. Finding it missing, I soon realized that I was no longer in Afghanistan. Slowly, reason returned to my consciousness.

The first sound that I heard was that of the rapid patter of my page boy running up the steps. Soon following were the heavy treads of a very large man. Adding to this sound was the wailing of a small child and the gentle tones of a woman's voice trying to comfort it.

I couldn't believe my eyes at the sight as they trooped through the door. Immediately behind my boy in buttons was a man I hadn't seen since Sherlock Holmes died in at the Reichenbach Falls. He was an exceedingly heavy man of great height, and very dignified dress and demeanor. It was my former friend's older brother, the honorable Mr. Mycroft Holmes. I was aghast. What business did this highly placed government official have with me? And who were the crying baby and the woman holding it?

In his normal august and diplomatic voice, Mr. Holmes declared, "Dr. Watson, please forgive me for disturbing you at this hour.

He sat down heavily on the divan and continued, "However, you are the only person in the world that I can turn to in such a private affair that threatens to bring great misery to one of our nation's most noble families and the continuation of its line. Read this note that was affixed to the infant's blanket."

The note, written in a scrawled cursive said, "My dear countess, I wish to inform you that if your husband does not accept elevation to the presiding officer of the House of Lords, I will not kill your daughter's child in the manner that this baby will soon suffer."

I replied, "Who is the countess that received this warning? Why have you contacted me in the matter? What do you expect me to do?"

The elder Holmes brother replied, "This is a matter that requires complete secrecy and confidence. We also need the services of an experienced medical man with the advanced degree of Doctor of Medicine. It has been my experience that when working with you and my brother, you were able to keep a secret and carry on whatever plans are required. What I want you to do are to determine why this child is dying and to find the person responsible, before the birth of the countess's grandchild."

"Sir," I replied, "That's a tall order. I am not a detective like Sherlock Holmes was. Also, I might need expert help in determining the cause of the infant's distress."

Just then, Dr. Verner appeared in the room. He said, "Who is this child and why is he crying?"

Then he realized the presence of Mycroft Holmes and said, "Mycroft, what is this? Why are you in our humble medical establishment?"

Mr. Holmes smiled at Dr. Verner and said, "Dr. Watson, you have the perfect helper."

Turning to Dr. Verner, he continued, "Hello Maurice. Dr. Watson will explain the issue. He will require your assistance. Now I must leave for important business of state."

And then, rising with great effort and turning to the woman he said, "Mrs. Black, please hand the child to the doctors for their examination. We are finished with her."

With that, the woman handed the still-crying infant to me and trod down the stairs following Mycroft Holmes and the scampering page boy.

Completely befuddled, I said, "Dr. Verner, please examine the child. Perhaps it has an infection."

Dr. Verner replied, "If we are concerned about an infectious disease, we had best examine it in my bacteriology laboratory. Please follow me."

I escorted him as he mounted the hallway stairs gently carrying the child, whose wailing had now ceased.

We entered the fourth level where Dr. Verner resided and performed his research and diagnoses. As his first action, Dr. Verner swabbed his examining table with 70% isopropyl alcohol. He removed the child's blanket and cloth wrapping, and laid the infant supinely on the now cleansed surface.

As he examined the infant, Dr. Verner asked me to get a pencil and pad and take notes. This is what he dictated. "We have a poorly nourished but clean baby girl approximately three days old. When she first arrived, she was crying very well. However, the crying decreased in intensity and has now stopped. On admission, she was drooling and showed drooping of her eyelids. The rapid movement of her arms and legs signifying distress had ceased, to be replaced by some tremors in her extremities. Her breathing was very labored. Now her arms were stiff in a paralytic state. Now they have become flaccid and lifeless and her breathing has stopped."

"Dr. Watson, please use your stethoscope and check for heart and lung sounds," he requested.

I did so and reluctantly confirmed his suspicions. The infant had died in our hands.

Dr. Verner said, "Now it is up to us to determine the cause of death. I know that it is a paralytic state that has led to respiratory failure. We must now attempt to define the cause. Only then can we try to determine who was cruel enough to do this to a helpless child and stop them from carrying out more such deaths, including the grandchild of an unnamed countess."

In the process, Dr. Verner quickly filled out the required death certificate indicating that the cause of death was paralysis, probably due to bacterial poisoning. He placed this on his desk for later sending.

Calling down the stairs Dr. Verner yelled, "Billy, I have an errand for you. Bring me all of the latest papers from the news agent down on the street as soon as possible. Then I may have another job for you, as a detective."

Billy, responding to the name that we always applied to our page regardless of his Christian name, proudly set out on his task, armed with a five pound note from Dr. Verner who told him to keep the change.

Then we set about our physical examination of the child. It was quickly ascertained that her arms and legs were completely flaccid. Everything else seemed normal except for a sweet smelling yellow sticky liquid in her nose and mouth.

The bacteriologist sterilized several metal loops in a Bunsen burner flame. He then placed several drops of the fluid from each body opening on several microscopic slides. On some, he added a clean cover slip. On several others, he spread the material in a thin film, gently heated them in a Bunsen flame, and placed a droplet of a blue dye on each and set them aside to dry.

Next he drew out the child's intestinal contents with a hypodermic syringe and needle after surgically exposing the intestines. He picked up eight laboratory mice from their cage and injected the child's intestinal contents into two each with a different route of administration: oral, intravenous, intraperitoneal, and subcutaneous.

Billy came running up the stairs carrying a pile of newspapers. Dr. Verner said, "Nice job, Billy."

Quickly scribbling on a piece of note pad, he handed it to Billy with four shilling coins saying, "Billy, I need you to go to this address and bring me a dog named Toby. Tell the proprietor that it's for Sherlock Holmes. The coins are for transportation, the dog rental, and for you. Come as quickly as you can. If you see any street Arabs, bring them with you. I may need their services."

Turning to me, Dr. Verner said, "let me examine the slides. It is obvious that the child has been paralyzed. I'm only aware of one agent that will act so quickly. I will examine the slides and inoculate blood agar Petri plates. But I don't expect much success in the cultivation except for the typical bacteria that always accompanies such an examination. Meanwhile, please glance through the papers and especially the social pages to see if any child of a countess is anticipating the arrival of a child."

Relegated to the position of a clerk, I reluctantly took the newspapers down the stairs to my reading light to follow orders. I would have much rather assisted in the medical exam, but I understood the importance of my task. After two hours of search, I was unable to find any reports of expected heirs to an Earl.

Upon returning to the bacteriology laboratory, I told Dr. Verner of my negative findings.

He replied, "I'm sorry, Dr. Watson. That would have been most helpful. However, I have other informal sources of information. Tomorrow we will call on Mr. Langdale Pike. He knows all of the gossip and events of the high social strata."

With that, Dr. Verner stated, "You need your rest. We will be very busy tomorrow. Get some sleep. I will consult with you in the morning after breakfast.'

Reluctantly, I walked down the stairs and poured myself a dram of cognac. Although my mind was racing with the developments of the evening, my consciousness had now recovered its vitality. A second drink aided my drowsiness, and I went o bed for a sound rest.

I awoke sometimes after 8:00 A.M. and was very hungry for the first time in weeks. I devoured a nourishing English breakfast of kippers, eggs, bacon American style, scrambled eggs, toast, and bitter orange marmalade, and two large mugs of black coffee. By 10:00 A.M. I was awake and ready for the day. What surprised me was that no patients had arrived for my services.

Then I heard the tread of Billy eagerly climbing the stairs to the upper level, the bark of a well-known dog who licked me fondly, and the patter of young feet that reminded me of Sherlock Holmes' Baker Street Irregulars. Curious, I took the stairs to Dr. Verner's facility to see him peering through a microscope as Billy and the five young ruffians awaited his attention.

Turning to Billy he said, "Billy, have Toby get the scent of a dead body in White Chapel and then follow him to whatever dead people you find. For any adults, notify the constables. If you find any children, have one of the lads contact me immediately."

Handing Billy a handful of shillings, Dr. Verner continued," Give each of the boys a shilling. I will give them a Guinea for alerting me to the death of a baby. Guard the body until I arrive."

Then he turned to me and said, "I suppose you are curious about the lack of patients. I took the liberty of rescheduling the common examinations for two days. I put a sign on the door for them to visit your neighbor in case of emergency. Now let us examine the slides."

Looking into the high power lens of the microscope at the stained slides I saw spare numbers of rod shaped bacteria. Using the very modern oil of emersion lens provided a sharper image of what were clearly bacilli. Similar images were found on all stained slides regardless of the source of material.

Dr. Verner said, "The similarity of the microbes from all of the body cavities indicates an identity of source. If they were truly at a singular infection site, there would be a much larger variety of morphology and one site would have much larger numbers. Whatever the viscous yellow liquid was, it was the media containing the microbes."

Then we examined the wet mounts. Unlike watery suspensions, the material still retained some degree of wetness.

Dr. Verner instructed, "Regard the large, irregular specks. This is clearly identifiable as soil, based on my experience with microscopic examination. Do you concur?"

Not knowing what to make of this I replied, "It is indeed a mystery to me. I would say that the fluid has all of the hallmarks of honey. But why would there be particles of dirt in honey, and why would that contaminated fluid be in the baby's mouth and nose?"

"This is really a diabolical coincidence," said Dr. Verner. "Let's now examine the slides I prepared from the mice. Look at this slide from the blood stream."

Looking at the stained slide, I visualized very large numbers of rod shaped bacteria in what should be a sterile environment. That the red blood cells had not hemolyzed indicated that destruction of the blood was not the cause of death. I was completely befuddled.

"Would it help if I told you that the symptoms in the mice during their death throes resembled that in the child?

Also, would it be instructive to know that injecting the blood and fecal contents from the mice caused immediate paralysis in the recipients? Had the rod-shaped bacteria been normal coliforms, death would have been more prolonged following a state of shock."

"My God, it's a toxin." I replied. "Could it be some form of toxigenic bacteria?" I asked.

"Yes," said Dr. Verner. "I have heard of cases like this in the latest research papers. It's caused by the contamination of honey by soil containing toxigenic bacteria. The disease is called botulism and only occurs from this source in babies. Some day we may learn how to cultivate and classify anaerobic bacteria. However, no one has yet been able to grow the microbe. They think that it might not tolerate air. Had the cause been a respiratory infection, the bacteria would most likely have been able to grow aerobically on blood, and most likely but not exclusively spherical in shape rather than bacilli."

Continuing, Dr. Verner said, "Several hours have passed. We must now take nourishment. All of this work has famished me. But I suggest that we forgo alcoholic beverages until we have completed our assignment."

We went together to our dining room to find that Mr. Holmes had sent over to us, at government expense, a wonderful luncheon of mixed fish and rolls. We set aside the wine for a later time, enjoying a fine Irish tea.

Dr. Verner said, "It is now time to go to Fleet Street to keep our appointment with Mr. Langdale Pike. Please get us a cab while I tell our cook and maid to notify any visitors to meet us there."

I employed a Brougham cab for our trip to visit Langdale Pike. I am not at liberty to reveal the name of the countess that is the topic of our account. That must be kept secret since her heirs still reside in their estate. However, we called on the government agent that was sent to follow us to place a guard over her home.

We had the opportunity to take a rest and smoke a Cuban cigar when a group of youngsters with a dog in tow approached us. Billy had taken his leave previously to bring over a constable telling him to wait for Dr. Watson and Dr. Verner. At Dr. Verner's direction, we all boarded a horse-drawn police bus and wended our way to the area in White Chapel in which one of the lads had found a dead baby. When we reached the site in this decrepit area of London, we were confronted by a peeved constable and an inspector. Fortunately the latter was an old friend, Tobias Gregson, known to me as one who had received the assistance of Mr. Sherlock Holmes on several occasions. The inspector greeted us warmly with handshakes, pleased that we were on a case. As we examined the child, we could see that he had honey in his mouth, and that his arms and legs were flaccid.

Dr. Verner turned to Inspector Gregson and asked, "We are on the track of a vicious killer, but credit for the case must eventually go to an agent of her majesty's government. Are you willing to help us capture and hold this villain until a government agent takes final charge?"

Gregson smiled and responded, "Dr. Watson, you and Mr. Holmes have done very right by me. You have helped solve several cases for which I was given the credit. There is no way that I could do otherwise than follow your request."

Looking at the inspector and me, my medical colleague declared, "We are on the track. This must have been an experiment. We will need to get more information. Dr. Watson, what I am about to ask may disturb you, but there is evidence that women who are too poor to maintain their infants will often sell them to baby brokers. Some are resold to work houses to become slaves to the owners of these establishments. Others are sold to dealers who supply dead bodies to medical schools for anatomical studies. The same people buy and sell adult cadavers and sometimes steal them from cemeteries. It is a dirty business."

I asked, "How does this help us?"

Dr. Verner replied, "Here comes Billy with Toby. I have no doubt that the hound will take us to a place where dead bodies are accumulated for sale. Billy has lived on the streets as a waif before Mr. Sherlock Holmes took him in. He will know the likely locations of these dealers in death. Between the page and the hound, we will locate the most likely sites."

Although the stench in the air was horrendous, our motley parade of Gregson and two constables, Dr. Verner, Billy, and Toby, four street Arabs, and I trooped on. Eventually we arrived at a yard surrounded by a high wooden fence. The enclosure was about 20 feet wide and 30 feet long. Although the gate was locked, Dr. Verner picked the mechanism as easily as an expert housebreaker. The odor of death was everywhere. However, there were no bodies or signs of habitation.

"This is not the place," said Dr. Verner. "Let's travel on."

The next location seemed more likely. It took Dr. Verner longer to negotiate the lock.

He stated, "This seems like a more professional location. The smell resembles that of a morgue or an anatomy lab. However, as we walked in we saw a sign that said 'Acme Meats.' It was a slaughter house. No luck there.

Finally, after much walking, as we left the poorest section to an area with local businesses, Toby barked very loudly. As we approached a brick building we saw a sign signifying that it was a storage unit for machinery. However, there was no doubting the smell coming from the open windows. It was clearly the smell of death.

Dr. Verner knocked on the door and declared "London Medical School. We are here for our order of heavy machinery."

As we heard heavy shoes walking away from the front room, another door opened. A hoarse voice called out, "Hold your horses matey. Be right with you."

Then the door banged shut and running steps could be heard along with the crying of an awakened infant. Less than a minute later, Gregson and the constables could be spotted leading a richly dressed middle aged bearded man around the side of the building. As one of the official police held the man in custody, Dr. Verner gently wrapped the child in his arms and covered his naked body with his coat for warmth.

Always on the ball, Billy said, "I'll get Mr. Holmes and return Toby."

As Billy left, Dr. Verner said, "We owe you our gratitude. I will raise your salary and get you a tutor so you can get a well deserved education."

Billy smiled, waved happily, and walked away.

While this was happening, I gave each of the waifs a gold sovereign and one shilling, and a hearty thank you.

All that was left was for Dr. Verner, the police officials, and I to inspect the facility. As we expected, on a table in the corner were several implements including knives, chains, and a lock picking kit. Alongside the objects of the man's craft were a pot of honey and a bag of dirt with a trowel in it. No confession would be needed.

Dr. Verner and I handed custody over to a man I recall as being Mr. Melas, who had indicated that he had been sent by Mycroft Holmes. So, as I thought, he was in the employ of her majesty's government. My hesitation was overcome when I saw Mr. Mycroft Holmes signaling from the back of a four wheeler. After Dr. Verner explained the results of our work to Mr. Holmes, the coach pulled away with killer in hand. As he left we promised to send a record of our activities to Mr. Melas for his evidence. We never heard of the case again, or what happened to the criminal. But we both received an invitation to dine with

Mr. Holmes and a certain gracious lady who presented each of us with a gold medallion for our Albert chains.

After this episode, Dr. Verner and I collected on our need for beverages, and we enjoyed several drinks of whiskey and fine cigars at Goldoni's.

I had allowed these events to pass from my consciousness. After the excitement of those few days, I returned to my brown study and dour mood. This was allayed by the events that occurred in the following week. I had returned from my daily visits to my patients, and as I climbed the stairs slowly, the only thing on my mind was tea and crumpets, and possibly a nap while I awaited unscheduled clients.

However, I was surprised to see the short, heavily muscled Greek man whom I knew as Mr. Melas. As I entered, he smiled, extended a hand for a firm shake, and said, "It is good to see you again, Dr. Watson. I hope my visit does not startle you."

I was pleased by the distraction of a visitor and for the excuse to imbibe a stronger beverage. "Please be seated. Would you care for some sherry?" said I, as I poured each of us a generous glass.

"Yes, thank you," he replied. "That will give us an opportunity to discuss a matter that has just come up."

Taking a sip of the fine sherry he said, "There has been additional movement on the baby toxicity situation. Although we caught the villain who carried out the original infanticides, the criminal behind these savage acts has not rested. We have evidence that he continues on his malevolent path."

"Please explain," I replied after I sipped some of the beverage.

"As an expert in mental disorders, you are aware that the perpetrator of such crimes will continue to repeat the same venue until he has accomplished his goal," Mr.

69

Melas stated. "It is what you psychologists would refer to as an *idée fixe*."

"Yes, of course," I replied. "Tell me how I can be of assistance."

Melas replied, "We fully expected another assault by intoxicated honey. Thus, we have been watching residents of the estate of the countess to determine if they visit the few purveyors of honey in London since we expect that to gain access to the child in question, the villain would be a resident. We planned to follow any customers of large quantities to see if they went towards the home of the countess. The criminal must have been aware of our attention to these venues. So far, no one has purchased honey and used it for criminal purposes."

I asked, "Then why have you contacted me?"

"We have received another warning note. But this one was not accompanied by a dead baby. The hand writing is exactly the same as that which accompanied the poisoned infant, and it appeared inside the house. Obviously, one of the residents is involved. Who would it be that can come and go to the Countess' domicile without arousing suspicion and would want the Earl to assume a high office in the government?"

"Don't you have agents better equipped to deal with this? I'm a doctor, not a secret agent," I replied.

"Ordinarily, that would be our modus operandi," stated Mr. Melas. "But if the criminal is in the government, he probably knows all of our operatives. On the other hand, you and Dr. Verner could be called into the house on a pretext of requiring medical assistance. There will be another person going in also. He will be posing as a purveyor of honey."

"What are you talking about?" I queried.

"Sometimes I put the cart before the horse. Let me explain. As I stated, we have been watching purveyors of honey to see where their clients go. None has gone to the house. However, look at these items in the paper."

The first item in the *Times* advertising pages stated, "Fresh honey for sale. No middle man. Delivered directly to your home. Answer ad in newspaper."

The second newspaper, a day later, said, "Very interested in honey sales. Please contact me by telegraph at this address."

Surprisingly, the address was the house of the countess.

Melas said, "The person purported to be delivering the honey is a student of mine in my Greek studies. He is a varsity boxer at Cambridge. Whoever accepts the delivery will be our prey."

On the following day, a mysterious hand-written note was received by Mr. Melas. It was written in the same cursive that had accompanied the infected bay.

Mr. Melas said, "This is really puzzling. Somehow the person desiring the honey has agents at the newspaper advertising department who informed our culprit where the advertisement came from. It smacks of an organized criminal organization. We must be on our guard."

The note said, "Deliver the honey this evening to the stables behind Dorchester House. Come alone."

I was stunned. Dorchester house is the domicile of the Earl of Dorchester, and has been the seat of that noble family for as far back as recorded history permits.

Mr. Melas continued, "Whoever this is probably knows the identity of many government agents. Hopefully, my anonymity is still in effect. But just in case the perpetuator doesn't identify me as the resident of the apartment to which he sent the note, but might recognize me on sight, I must not be in his view. Dr. Watson, I must call on you to be the intermediary of the honey transfer. My men and I will then step in and capture the purchaser. Are you willing to do this?"

"Of course," I replied. "I will do whatever is needed to save the innocent child for such a malicious act as poisoning."

That evening, near sunset, I dressed in one of Sherlock Holmes' costumes and took on the persona of an itinerant peddler. Every large city has its busy areas served by public transportation and its environs are well known to the public. However, there are areas where only the highly placed individuals and their person servants and occasional workers are permitted to enter. In these vast estates, the well born live their lives of seclusion and luxury without need to interact with the lower classes of society. Such was the Dorchester estate.

To avoid suspicion, I traveled by a circuitous route avoiding expensive means of transportation; the area to which I was traveling was not served by public transportation, and I didn't want to be identified by a carriage driver. After leaving the privately acquired dog cart that I had used to reach my destination, I wended my way through the side alleys between the trees to a mews at the rear of the estate. It is through the mews, where horses are groomed, that I could gain access to the stables.

It had grown dark. The only sounds were the nocturnal birds and the animals seeking their prey or companionship. As I slowly and fearfully entered the stable, I could tell that the excrement of the horses had been removed and that the air was free of the normally fetid odor. All of the horses had been removed for their grooming. Darkness and fear made me receptive to auditory stimuli and my sense of smell was alerted. As I stood in the darkened stable, I could detect the odor of sandalwood fragrance approaching me. Also, the zipping sound of corduroy knickers signaled the approach of an expensively dressed rider in expensive gear.

Then I was blinded by a high intensity electric torch. "Dr. Watson," a familiar high baritone whiny voice assaulted my ears. "I would know you anywhere. I'm on to your tricks! Well, hand over the honey and I might not kill you!"

"Sir Killian," I replied. "What have you to do with this?"

I was surprised that such a high member of society would be involved in a malevolent plot involving the death of children. Not wishing to facilitate his deed, I pulled the beaker of honey from my pocket and slowly let it slip from my fingers.

"No, he yelled, and dove down to catch the precious fluid before it was irretrievably lost. As he bent over, he was immediately grabbed by the strong arms of two government agents hiding in the dark. In the light of their lanterns I could see, brandishing a knife, a woman I recalled as being named Sophie. She pointed the way for the criminal to vacate the premises. Without speaking, the government officials led the villain silently away as he sobbed softly.

I was left alone until Dr. Verner appeared to conduct me back to our facility. Neither of us was made aware of the government's plan for the killer. The next time I saw Mr. Mycroft Holmes, I tried to broach the subject, but he refused to answer. It wasn't until weeks later that I knew why Sir Killian wanted the Earl to reject the position of leader of the House of Lords, and always assumed that such affairs of government were well kept secret.

It had been a miserable day, wet and damp. It never rally rained, but a constant drizzle and slight chill did little to elevate my spirits. As I entered my sitting room, I was effusively greeted by my partner Dr. Verner. He smiled and offered me whiskey and soda to warm up.

He said, "Dr. Watson, I'm pleased that you have arrived. Sit here with me by the fire. I think that I have news that will please you: a solution to our last adventure.

But first, I want to celebrate our accomplishment with you as well as my recent birthday."

After removed my damp coat, I toweled my face. As I sat next to him, Dr. Verner handed me a cigar. He then refreshed my drink. I could see that he was in no mood to get to the point.

He then said, "Come join me in a festive meal so that we will be better able to digest the news of past events. It is time that we get to know each other better and become friends."

Although I was anxious for him to get to the point, the odor of a luxurious repast brought in by a caterer convinced me to await his decision to continue the tale on his own terms. The excellent rare roast and potatoes, accompanied by many glasses of red wine served to lighten my mood. After dining, we retreated to the fire side for port and coffee.

Dr. Verner turned to me with a smile said, "I feel that our joint adventure has brought us closer together. I would like us to become friends since we share mutual interests, and are often in close contact with each other. It is getting unhandy to keep calling you Dr. Watson. Would you mind if we were on first name terms? I could call you John, if you approve."

Since I was fully agreeable to this sense of comradery I replied, "That would be fine. However, my few friends call me James. That started in school when my teachers discovered my middle name is Hamish, the Scottish equivalent of James. There were so many Johns in the school that it was more definitive to be known as James. I really didn't want to be called Hamish, even though I was educated in Scotland."

"Please call me Maurice, my given name. This appellation stems from the fact that my forbears were of French descent. Although we have anglicized out surname from Vernet to Verner, we still keep the French for our

74

Christian names in honor of our relatives still residing in France. My predecessors are the famous French artists."

I replied, "I noticed that you and Mycroft Holmes were on first name terms. Is he a close friend of yours?"

Verner countered, "No. But we are distant cousins. Mycroft is also descended on his maternal side from the Vernet family."

Then gazing at me with a serious mien, my new friend Maurice said, "Now that we have shared an adventure, and that I plied with you with food and beverages, we have become comrades. Now I have another association to offer you."

This made me very suspicious. Was he asking me to join him in a business venture?

I was relieved when he said, "I would like you to consider joining me and some as my colleagues as occasional intelligence agents for the British Government. You must realize by now that I as well as Melas and the woman calling herself Sophie are also agents, and that Mycroft Holmes is our supervisor. Melas and Sophie are employees of the government, but several others are called upon as necessary. Also the reason that Sherlock Holmes was asked to provide several services to the country, at Mycroft's request, was the fact that he also served in that capacity. For our services, we are not financially compensated, and there may be danger. However, we perform these activities in a spirit of British patriotism. Our government does not favor having a full time espionage agency, so we are called upon as needed to fill the gap undercover of our real occupations. Would you agree to join us in this endeavor?"

I smiled, clasped his hand in a firm grip, and said, "There is nothing I would rather do than serve the kingdom in the capacity that you suggest."

Maurice walked over to the chairs by the fire and beckoned me to join him in a whiskey and soda. Thus seated, we toasted each other quietly.

Then Maurice said, "Now that you have agreed to join our cause, I feel that I can inform you of the final outcome of the honey poisoning case."

I replied, "That would be most instructive. I never understood why such a highly regarded gentleman as Sir Killian would be behind that. He has money, women, and prestige. What more could he want? Is he an heir to the Earl's estate and title?"

Maurice replied, "Although financial gain may seem to be Sir Kalian's motivation, it really has to do with his obsession with bees."

I was taken aback that something as trivial as a love of our apiarian friends would drive someone to infanticide and blackmail.

I said, "I don't understand the connection."

Maurice replied, "The Earl was a leader of a group who favored industrial development of the South Downs. Sir Killian, on the other hand, was involved in apiary growth and research in a plot of land in the area. To him, it was essential to maintain his establishment at all costs, even if it led to the death of infants and a threat to the Countess. He feared that had the Earl become leader of the Lords, he would deprive Killian of his facility."

I replied, "I understand perfectly. My studies in mental disorders would lead me to agree with your diagnosis. However, where did Killian develop the knowledge to carry out his plan to poison the honey with toxigenic microbes? This is certainty new science."

Maurice replied, "Sir Killian had attended medical school until he was dismissed for trading in kidnapped children. Since that time, the criminal element often used his nefarious services to commit murders that could not be detected. While in school, his studies on methods of murder

76

instructed him in the use of honey laced with bacterial spores to provide infant's bodies for his trade. But fortunately, his reign in this field is now at an end. The land in question would never have been developed for industrial purposes. Mycroft has taken over the coastline as an area to spy on the transit of French and German ships. He has maintained the bee keeping operation as a cover. In addition to the apiarist, he has employed an agent named Martha to surviel the navigation lanes and send reports to his office."

"But what of Sir Killian?" I asked. "Where is he held captive and will he be tried for his crimes?"

Replied Maurice, "He is serving a life term of hard labor as the humble beekeeper for the Queen in the South Downs, a far cry from his previous existence as an honored noble."

I replied, "We must be careful what we wish for. Sir Killian's obsession to pursue apiary science at all costs had terrible repercussions. His impulses led him to perform horrendous crimes resulting in his loss of wealth and privilege and sentencing to a servile existence as a humble servant in a desolate location. To him this is a life worse than death."

Dr. Watson and the Adventure of the Pearls of Death [1]

Maurice Verner and Alicia, his beautiful blonde-haired wife, were enjoying their drinks – 25-year-old single malt Scotch, after a laborious day. Maurice had just done the finishing touches on a review article on the development of antibacterial agents for drug-resistant microbes. His Ph.D. in microbiology and many years as a consultant in antibiotic discovery for several pharmaceutical companies around the globe had prepared him for this venture. Alicia, on the other hand, had just finished editing her latest Sherlockian pastiche for the publishing company that was one of the Verner family businesses.

Maurice picked up the printed adventure of Dr. John Watson that Uncle Horace had presented him with the previous week. He had recently finished reading "The Case of the Deadly Honey," and was now ready for the next adventure involving his physician ancestor and Dr. John H. Watson during the great hiatus.

"Maurice," said Alicia with a cute smile, "I see by the title of the story that it involves jewelry; I want to read it next. But don't forget, we're meeting at the Rattlesnake Club to celebrate Uncle Horace's birthday. Aunt Juliet said not to be late, since your brothers and cousins will be there also."

Maurice Verner settled down to read Dr. Watson's account as he awaited the arrival of his relatives for the short ride to the hotel.

He hoped the story would also feature his physician ancestor, as had the adventure concerning the contaminated honey that brought about botulism in infants. He began to read:

I was vaguely aware of the squishing and splashing sounds that were interwoven with the rhythmic rattling of the wheels of my Hansom cab. They were the only remnants of the torrential rain and gale force winds that had deluged London for the past week. The storm had been replaced by a clear bright, moon-filled evening and a chill breeze. The cold wind and clear sky presaged the coming of the winter season. I deeply regretted my lack of foresight as I sat shivering, protected only by my professional attire and a light blanket. The changing climatic conditions and the strenuous efforts required to quell the raging influenza epidemic had conspired to exacerbate both of my war wounds. The bouncing of the coach did not help the situation. My shoulder and leg throbbed with pain. Now, bone tired and aching, I was destined for a lonely evening devoid even of the comfort of my deceased wife's company. The fact of her recent death following that of my only friend, Sherlock Holmes, added to my ennui.

My day had started at early sunlight. I was summoned by the servant of Mrs. Cecil Forrester, the woman who had taken such good care of my sweet Mary after she returned to London. Mrs. Forrester had taken Mary in as her governess after the discovery that her father had disappeared forever. Upon entering the luxurious apartment, I immediately noticed a man on the verge of death. I barely recognized the well-known Lord Herbert McFallow. Instead of the virile hero of many victorious battles in the service of the Empire, he was a thin and weak shadow of his former self. His dagger-like dark beard was now white and laying flat on his breast as he lay motionless on the couch that was his resting place. I quickly recognized that he was not suffering from influenza, a disease with which I was very conversant. When I had seen him only two days before, he had vague signs of a mild respiratory illness – perhaps a cold. It did not appear to require my attention. Summoned back the nest afternoon, I noted that the patient was still ill, but there were no further symptoms of a cold. There was no runny nose, sneezing, or nasal congestion. He did complain of a sore nose and general weakness. Missing were typical signs of influenza. I ticked off the missing signs of that disease: shortness of breath, chest pain, coughing up bloody sputum, mental confusion, or convulsions. What did strike me as odd was the strange odor that emanated from his body. It was like something that I had never encountered before.

If I were to help him, I would require the services of a specialist. Fortunately, the home was equipped with a telephone, enabling me to contact Dr. Verner, a colleague who is a specialist in bacteriology in his clinic at St. Bart's. As I awaited his arrival, Mrs. Forrester kindly provided me with a cup of coffee and a pastry to tide me over. As Dr. Verner finally arrived, Lord Herbert rapidly succumbed to his illness. He summoned all of his resources as his body attempted to stave off certain death. This obviously was not a symptom of influenza, and indicated that the suffering man would not last much longer, as he slowly sunk back into his moribund state. Dr. Verner took over the examination of the body. I stayed briefly to fill him in. He then shooed me away with a push of his hands so that I could care for my other patients who were awaiting my services.

Maurice said, on my departure, "I will need to examine the patient, take specimens, and carry them back to my laboratory in our shared quarters. There may be a serious epidemic that would spread if we don't diagnose it and prevent its spread. Meet me in our quarters when you have completed your rounds."

I endured the long ride back to my apartments, nestled above my now prosperous practice. My mind reflected back to the recent past events. I lay back, resigned to my fate, and shrugged my shoulders as I accepted my sorry plight. Sorrow and despair for those whom I had been unable to heal and had died despite my best efforts, were followed by anger and frustration at the limits placed upon me by the lack of therapeutic measures available to thwart the dread disease of influenza.

Then, a gentle smile flowed over my features as I remembered the kindly face of my lovely wife Mary and our parting conversation as I left the Lower Camberwell domicile of Mrs. Cecil Forrester. I could still see the drawing room door closing behind Mrs. Forrester as she, in robe and slippered feet, weakly retired for the evening. Then, we were alone together at last. My wife Mary, after rising on her toes and gently kissing me on the special spot just below my right eye, and using her private pet name said: "My dear James. How thoughtful and accommodating of you to allow me to tend to my former employer in her time of need, with both her and her husband dreadfully ill. They have been the only parents I have known since the death of my poor father, and they have always treated me as a beloved member of their family."

To which I smiled and replied: "I would not want it to be otherwise, my sweet angel of mercy. I will miss you terribly. I expect to share many a day with you, and that knowledge of our continued companionship will keep me happy until you return home to my side."

And that was the last conversation we had before her untimely death from pneumonia two days later.

Finished with my reverie of recently past events, I permitted my mind to drift back to previous adventures with my former friend. I recalled with glory and pain my military adventures in the service of the Queen, my subsequent return to England, and my momentous first meeting with my friend and erstwhile colleague Sherlock Holmes. I smiled as I contemplated the many interesting discussions that we had, usually in the afternoon after tea, concerning the changes in weather patterns associated with the tilt of the earth, various athletic competitions, literature, music, and philosophy.

I was looking forward to my schedule becoming less hectic in the near future due to the end of the influenza and cold season previously brought on by the cold and damp and the close personal contact that followed the desire of people to crowd together avoiding the rain. As I arrived home, I barely recalled the death of Lord Herbert. The activities soon following my arrival would quickly refresh my memory of this event.

I looked forward to seeing my new friend and colleague Dr. Maurice Verner and to determine the fate of my erstwhile patient, the subject of his examination. That would be followed by a comfortable fire, a nip or more of the contents of the spirit case and the gasogene, a fine cigar from the coal-scuttle. An interesting dialogue about the latest discoveries in bacteriology was just the medicine I required to restore my spirits, and allay my dread of spending yet another lonely night with none but the servants for company. My pleasure was doubled as I spotted the light glowing in the facade of the top level of our quarters.

"Good!" I thought, "Maurice is both at home and still awake. I will learn the outcome of his examination of Lord Herbert."

As I labored up the three-flights of steps, which seemed like miles to my bone-weary and pained body, Maurice Verner's baritone voice rang out, "James, my new colleague, I would know that tread anywhere! You are just in time to join me in a celebration as I reach the climax of another difficult and challenging case. There is something I must show you while we await a response to my message. Then we must be off on a long carriage ride."

These were the last words that I expected to hear or wanted to hear. But, how characteristic it was of my new friend. In many ways, he reminded me of Sherlock Holmes: tall, wiry thin, very athletic, and sharp as a tack. It had been thus from our meeting at St. Bart's in the newly installed bacteriology lab, and had never changed. Gone were the dreams of pleasant, cozy surroundings and relaxing conversation. The meditative, philosophical Verner that I had envisioned was replaced by Verner, the energetic infectious disease investigator.

"What have I gotten myself into now?" I asked myself. Realizing that it was too late to turn back, I continued my slow progress to Verner's abode.

Then I saw Maurice Verner. The lanky figure of the man was bending almost in half to accommodate the height of the table that supported the device through which he was now looking. His lean, hawk-nosed, angular facial features were somewhat softened by the beaming smile that lightened his usually dour, clean shaved countenance.

"Come see my new high-powered microscope!" shouted Verner, looking at the strange black instrument as a child would gaze at a new toy at Christmas. "It is the same as that utilized by the famous German physician, Herr Professor Dr. Robert Koch, to study the life cycle of the tubercle bacillus. Certainly you have heard of his great discoveries!" blurted Verner. "It can magnify images several hundredfold larger than they really are! There are, as yet, very few in England, although they have become popular in Germany. Look through the top lens and very, very slowly focus by turning the large cylinder. But, whatever you do, do not touch the slide with your fingers! It may be a deadly error. Tell me, what do you see?"

As I slowly and timidly followed Verner's instructions, a very strange sight resolved itself out of the mist. Before my eyes was revealed the image of tangled, sinuous threads. Glistening in the center of the threads were evenly spaced opalescent, shining ovals. The appearance was that of a treasure box filled with strings of identical, lovely pearls.

I said, "Maurice, what is this? This is a beautiful, priceless sight that nature has prepared for us, is it not?"

"I am afraid, my poetic friend, that this object that you so admire is the mechanism for a diabolic, murderous scheme by a highly intelligent criminal. However, we must travel far to the other side of London, should we wish to learn the identity of the brilliant villain," said Maurice, very concernedly, "or additional murders may result. Before we leave, however, you must also look at the same slide in a standard high-powered objective, one that you are more conversant with."

My practiced eye gazed at the more familiar microscopic field and quickly announced, "Maurice that is the bacillus of anthrax. There can be no mistaking it. But what has this to do with your current case? Certainly there is no mystery to be attached to the affliction that is somewhat prominent in butchers, wool sorters, and others who handle potentially infected animal products. It is very easy to diagnose from a patient history and clinical grounds. The name anthrax refers to the coal-black cutaneous lesions that characterize this disease."

"James, let us continue our observations further with more scientific evidence. Look in the low-powered microscope, it is also very illustrative."

Quickly focusing the device to which I was most accustomed, as a result of my medical training, I saw a mass of some brownish vegetative fibers in which were embedded a few strands of hair. "Is that tobacco?" I asked, "and animal hairs? What a very strange combination of items."

Retorted Verner: "I see that your mind has been opened to unlikely possibilities as a result of our shared adventures. Yes, you are correct. Not only are the hair and tobacco part of the threads that tie together the available evidence in this case, but the material on the slide that you have previously viewed as well. In association with your suspicions voiced in a recent conversation that we had, these findings form a link to the discovery of the murderer of Lord Herbert McFallow, and possibly others. Now, I see that you are weary. Since we have time before a response takes us to our early morning vigil, I suggest that you rest yourself in front of the fire, and enjoy one of the cigars that I had imported from Tampa, Florida, in the United States. Here is a glass of whiskey and soda to accompany your relaxation while we chat about this matter."

After drawing deeply on the cigar, and taking a long drink of the warming beverage, I finally continued our conversation: "Maurice, how is that possible? What did I say that led you to this line of reasoning?"

"My dear fellow, it was you who suspected that the recent death of Lord Herbert may not have been the result of the ongoing influenza epidemic. In your phone call you stated that the respiratory symptoms that preceded his death appeared to be dissimilar to those encountered with influenza or a simple cold, or anything else that you were familiar with. Also, there were signs of toxic manifestations not found in those diseases. In your judgment, and from your personal experience with the current epidemic, there were subtle nuances that led you to call me into the case. You, yourself, stated that the signs of shock and the rapid onset of lethality ruled out influenza in your mind. You suspected foul play, poisoning."

"Yes, Maurice, it was due to my recent experiences and my hearkening to the teachings of my professor of surgery at Edinburgh, Dr. Joseph Bell, whom you appear to emulate in many respects."

To which Verner replied: "Of all living men, his teachings provide the best examples of logical deduction. But, we digress. Do you recall my examination of your patient?"

"Yes, Maurice, you crawled all around the body on your hands and knees looking at everything carefully with your hand lens. Then, you looked all around his mouth with a small mirror after taking a whiff of his breath to detect the presence of poison, and then you looked into his nose."

"Yes," replied colleague, who then asked, while exhaling fumes from his recently lighted pipe, "Did I do anything that you have never seen me do before?"

"Why Maurice, now that I think of it, you took a scraping from his nose. I never saw you do that before."

"That is quite true, James. You must take your clews where you find them. I am always puzzled why you do not ask why, when I do something different. A curious scientist would have wanted to look and see just what was in Lord Herbert's nose that aroused my inquisitiveness."

"But Maurice, there were no cutaneous lesions to point to anthrax, and the history of the illness would tend to rule out men of the character of Lord Herbert, who has never been accused of doing any physical labor in his life. What is the relationship between your demonstrations and the death of that noble gentleman?"

"That is the deviousness of the whole incident," replied Verner. "Someone with your forthright and gentlemanly character would have a difficult time connecting these events. But, I both suffer from and am assisted by an advanced case of cynicism where every action is suspect, no matter how unconnected and innocent they may seem. Also, to my advantage, I trust no one, except, of course, you and my cousin Mycroft."

"Are you proposing that the tobacco was a means of transporting the bacillus of anthrax to Lord Herbert, and the animal hair was the source of the microbe? What a terrible yet ingenious plot," I continued. "Only a very evil scientist could have devised this scheme."

"Yes," responded Maurice Verner, while lighting another pipe full of tobacco, "You are probably correct in your hypothesis. An additional slide revealed that the

Lord's snuff was laced with lamb's wool. We will need some further evidence, however, to confirm our theory."

Before I could reply, a sound of young feet rapidly padding up the stairs heralded the appearance of a very dirty, very smelly, and very scruffy young street Arab. Verner said quickly to me, "Ah, one of my worthy associates has a message for me. Our wait is over. We must now hurry." Turning to the lad, he continued: "I trust that a conveyance awaits to take us to the end of our search."

A positive nod from the street urchin brought a shilling coin into his hands and he sped off, rapidly followed by Verner with me being pulled along as I attempted to don the large baggy coat tossed to me by my companion.

I asked," Where are we off to?"

"I do not know," shouted Verner over the loud clatter of wheels and the hoof beats of the two galloping steeds that rapidly pulled our four-wheeler through the empty, cold streets of London. "Our lad will guide the driver, but I suspect the final destination will be in a slaughterhouse or tanners, possibly on Aldgate Street or Harrow-Alley."

Now wide awake, all pain and drowsiness were removed by the adrenaline coursing through my circulation. I still shivered, but not with the cold, which was allayed by the warm clothing supplied by Verner from his vast supply of costume over garments, but by the thrill of the chase. It was good to be back in the hunt with my friend! It was good to share another exciting adventure with Maurice Verner!

"Maurice, I really missed our little excursions together. Thank you for enabling me to accompany you on yet another."

In response to that statement, Maurice Verner handed me folded newspaper clippings and a telegram.

"Regard these, friend Watson, while I plan our course of action as we note the area to which our journey takes us. I will need to have my wits about me, and devise an extemporaneous plan of attack, depending upon our surroundings."

"It was just like Verner to thrust information on me, rather than simply answering my straightforward questions," mused I, *sotto voce*. Continuing, I thought, "Verner is always trying to get me to think like him. Doesn't he realize that he is of a rare breed? In many ways he is just like Sherlock Holmes."

With great difficulty, due to the violent swaying and bouncing of the carriage, I was barely able to read the following item from the agony column of *The Times* for that morning:

To the Tobacconist: I require some more of your special snuff. Please deliver three bags full to the usual location. Little Bo Peep.

Preceding that date were several other private notices of the same sort. "What could it mean?" I thought, glancing at my inscrutable companion who was placidly peering straight ahead, his pipe firmly clenched between his teeth, his mind completely focused on the problem at hand. I knew that any attempts at conversation or questioning would be ignored when my friend presented that visage to the world, and resigned myself to a silent journey. Then I turned my attention to the telegram, which, surprisingly enough was from Germany:

Dr. Verner, description of symptoms, clinical signs, laboratory findings confirm your suspicions. Await further word. Most interested. R. Koch

The last, of course, I understood fully. It had to do with the identity of the microbe, an identity that Dr. Verner had confirmed minutes ago in his laboratory. Still somewhat puzzled, as I mused about the full import of all that had occurred that night and into the early morning, the four-wheeler lurched to a sudden stop.

"Quick, James, we must follow this lad to see where he leads us!" whispered Verner, as he drew me forcefully from the conveyance to the ground. "We must make haste; we do not know when our prey will arrive. I am certain that he suspects nothing. I suggest that you be careful where you step, though. And do not remove your gloves for any reason. And wear this scarf around your nose and mouth for further protection."

As we watched, the boy was joined by an older one, clothed in gloves and scarf, who, as disreputable appearing as his companion, seemed to be in a command position. Rapidly, the street was filled by other similarly clad, silent boys, who seemed to flow endlessly from the shadows into the bright moonlight that was just giving way to a pale dawn. Slipping out of the alley to their left, another furtive youngster quickly took Verner's hand, and the trio proceeded into the darkness, around two corners and into the back door of an establishment smelling of dead animals and their feces.

"Be very quiet, James, we do not wish to apprehend our man here. We need to follow him to his delivery point to catch the criminals at the next higher level in their enterprise."

Joined by a second lad, the four of us furtively followed the dim lantern glow into the cavernous slaughterhouse. Turning another corner, we spotted a door framed in bright light on the other side of the immense room. Closing the window on the lantern, Verner led our assembled patrol towards the source of light, like moths to a flame. As we slowly inched our way through the silently opened doorway into the blinding early morning sunlight pouring in from the window, we could perceive nothing of interest. Then, from behind, came the unmistakable dull thud of a rifle being cocked. Apparently startled by the sound, the figure of a man, with a long, sharp object clutched in one hand, rose up in their sight and was framed against the glare of the sun at the level of the eastern horizon. The bleating of a lamb indicated that a fearful animal was grasped by the man armed with the blade.

"No! Don't fire!" shouted Verner, "Hold your fire or all is lost!"

But his plea was useless. The roar of a powerful rifle reverberated in our ears as the human figure fell to the floor. The heavy treads of large feet heralded the entrance of a plain- clothed detective and two burly constables into the room.

"You ruined everything;" shouted Verner to the police. "Why did you shoot him? He would harm no one with his blade, it was only a scissors. And he could lead us to his superior."

"But Dr. Verner," said the inspector, "We are not armed. It was not us who killed the man."

"I am very sorry that I accused you and your men Inspector; please forgive me," Verner replied contritely.

"We all make mistakes don't we, Dr. Verner, even famous consulting doctors," concluded the policeman, with a sarcastic tone that one would use to a recalcitrant child, a slight smile on his face.

"Alas, then, we have been outsmarted," Verner continued in a voice so quiet that only we I could understand his words. "Leaving nothing to chance, the master criminal behind the enterprise arranged for his agent to be spied upon and eliminated to avoid capture. That was his insurance policy against betrayal. However, there is nothing we can do to remedy the situation, and I am certain that the killer has left the premises and will never be found. James, I note that you have rushed to provide medical assistance to our quarry. How does he fare?"

I glumly replied, "He is dead Maurice. We will get no further information from him."

The glow of the bright sunlight revealed an unusual scene. We were in the midst of a dirty slaughterhouse. On the floor lay a short, stout, unkempt, unshaven blonde-haired man of about twenty years of age. Next to where the man was lying was the only living four-legged animal in attendance. It was a sick, scraggly lamb, partly shorn of its wool. Nearby, on the floor, were a pair of shears and a basket that contained the wool that was no longer attached to the body of the animal.

"Why, that man is Melbourne, the son of our tobacconist!" I exclaimed. "What the deuce is he doing here? What is he up to?"

Turning my way, Verner very quietly said, "He or someone in his father's employ was the logical candidate as the assassin or his helper. I knew the source of the snuff by the label left on the container in Lord Herbert's possession. And the account book that I found in the shop, among the man's things, now completes the picture. Let us continue the discussion after I have dismissed the official representatives of the law."

"Gentlemen," continued Maurice more loudly, addressing the policemen and then favoring me with a wink of his eye, "You may remove the body. I think that the case of the phantom wool gatherer is solved. I suggest that you remove the body and file your report. Take the body to the morgue so that I can do a post-mortem exam.

After the police had left, and the Irregulars were dismissed with their earnings, I turned to Verner and in a conspiratorial voice remarked, "It will be interesting to see how the police and newspapers will report the crime of phantom wool gathering that has not as yet been brought to their official attention."

"Yes, my friend, let us now turn to matters at hand," said Verner, his eyes still twinkling with silent amusement from the joke that he had just perpetrated on the Official Police.

"It appears that the young gentleman, once a medical student, but now fallen to a lower level, has collaborated in a series of murders. I am certain that the names in his book will not reveal to us the clients who used his services to carry out assignations behind the veil of the influenza epidemic. They are no doubt obfuscated by a secret code. But, thank you for initiating our most interesting case. Your perceptive medical skills were essential in beginning the process of deducing the rest of the puzzle from the pieces that revealed themselves to my inquiry. That set into motion a series of events which eventually led to his unfortunate death. Let us now return to our lodgings where we can rest and resolve any outstanding issues."

Once again in the familiar surroundings of our medical offices and lodgings, I finally realized that all of the pain and fatigue that led me to seek quiet solace in these chambers had been eradicated by the exciting events that had ended less than an hour ago. I knew that I had earned a good night's sleep from my endeavors, but that my reward would not come until my mind was made easy by the discourse from Dr. Verner that was certain to follow the maddeningly prolonged routine now underway: the cleaning of the pipe, the filling of the pipe with tobacco, the lighting of the pipe, letting the fire go out, tamping it just so, and finally, carefully making certain that the entire surface was evenly lighted. Only then did Dr. Maurice Verner commence the discourse long awaited from my new friend and associate:

"Well, my good friend and patient companion, I perceive that you have, for the most part, penetrated the solution to our little problem from the evidence that I have so far revealed to you and from what you have seen tonight. Are there any questions that you wish to ask me to assist you in its elucidation?"

"Yes, Maurice, what is it that you saw in Lord Herbert's nose that initiated your studies in this matter?" replied I. "What could it have been that led you from Lord Herbert's nose to a filthy slaughterhouse in the worst part of London? And what do the newspaper clippings and telegrams have to do with it?"

"Well, would it help if I told you that there was a pustule in his nose?"

I looked up and nodded my head in affirmation. All was now clear. "Of course," I replied, "The wool-laden tobacco was the means of delivery of the bacillus. The animal hair that was mixed with the tobacco must have been from an infected lamb such as the one we encountered in tonight's excursion. The tobacco and hair were scraped from Lord Herbert's nose, and I assume that the same material was found in his snuff box."

"You are quite correct in your assessment. Now let me tie all of the facts together with the information that you only had a chance to glance at, into a uniform narrative, and you tell me if you agree, or if I have overlooked any points that require further elucidation," Verner said.

He then began a recitation in the style of a medical professor. "Let us start anew. That Lord Herbert died from a respiratory infection other than influenza, or possibly even poisoning, was an hypothesis derived from your clinical observations. For that, you have my gratitude for providing me with a case to drive away the ennui of the last few days that were filled with constant rain and no cases worthy of my attention. Even the activities of members of the criminal class were curtailed by the horrendous weather. Also, there were no significant outbreaks of infectious disease that required my intervention .To continue my discourse: an observation of the body revealed an unusual lesion in the nose. When I later looked at the nasal scrapings in my low-powered microscope, I saw the presence of inflammatory cells, and some tobacco and animal hair. My microscopic analysis of these items was simplified by the fact that I am preparing monographs on both topics. It was clearly a mixture of lamb's wool and a type and cut of tobacco only used in snuff. Not only that, but I could see, in my examination, that it was identical to that purveyed by my personal tobacconist, and few others. Is it clear so far, James?"

"Yes, absolutely, please continue, while I help myself to another excellent cigar," I said, lighting the cigar and then puffing easily as I sat comfortably in the overstuffed chair, patiently awaiting the continuation of the scholarly exposition.

Verner went on: "The next thing that I did was sample Lord Herbert's snuff supply, and confirm the source of the suspected product. I sent our street Arabs out for snuff samples. A sampling of the products at the few stores revealed no contaminated snuff on their premises. The contaminated snuff was solely localized to Mrs. Forrester's abode. This meant that the material had to be placed at the victim's home by someone after the snuff had been especially prepared elsewhere for delivery. And, that it was done deliberately for the purpose of murder, not as a result of inadvertent contamination at the manufacturers."

After going through the pipe ritual again, the recitation continued thus: "What would tie together the snuff, sheep's wool, a pustulant lesion, and a respiratory infection? A perusal of the medical references in my office seemed to point to wool sorter's disease as the most logical solution. Certainly, if wool sorters can be infected by inhaling the wool of diseased sheep as they process it, couldn't the same material, carefully and continuously placed in an individual's nose achieve the same end? And wouldn't the symptoms emulate those of influenza to all but the well trained and experienced observer like you? What a diabolical plot!"

With that, my face lit with appreciation of my friend's detective skills. I expostulated: "Maurice, your ability to tie these diverse aspects together is marvelous. Once you gave me the available information, I was able to see that Lord Herbert died of anthrax. But to know what to look for to discern that the wool sorter's disease was conveyed to the site of infection by the continuous application of snuff laced with the wool of infected sheep is excellent! A marvelous deduction! My hat is off to you. I fully understand the microscopic pearl necklace and the German telegram. But, the Baker Street Irregulars and the mysterious newspaper clippings, what part did they play?"

"James Watson, you know my methods. To confirm the identity of the infecting microbe, I perused a telegram from Herr Professor Dr. Robert Koch for information on cultivating and identifying the causative bacillus. The high-power microscope, purchased previously at his suggestion, revealed identical images from gelatin cultivations of the microbe from the nasal scraping, the snuff sample, hair from infected sheep, and finally, a specimen I had obtained from Dr. Koch himself several weeks ago. These are the deadly images of pearl necklaces that you so admired. One drop of a suspension containing them would kill a man in 24 hours. Also, the spores will remain infective in the snuff supply for many years due to the resistance of the spores to environmental conditions. Dr. Koch's telegram merely confirmed the validity of pursuing my observations, as did your microscopic analysis. But how do I find the individual personally responsible for this heinous crime, and how do I trap him into revealing my nefarious activities? I suspected, immediately, that the answer may lie within the establishment of only a very few tobacconists who purvey this particular blend of snuff, but I needed to perform one of my little experiments to test this tentative hypothesis. There was no other plan that I could pursue, since no suspect product was found at any of the locations. By the way, I seem to have purchased a large amount of snuff, would you like to have some for yourself? Anyway, hoping that standard means of communication were used to order the lethal snuff, I scoured every newspaper for the last several weeks leading to the death of Lord Herbert, and found in *The London Times* a series of notices from the 'Little Bo Peep' to the 'tobacconist.' I theorized that 'Little Bo Peep' was actually the person who arranged the murders, and that he was looking for lost sheep, in the form of 'special snuff.' In order to locate these individuals, I placed the advertisement that drew 'the tobacconist' out. I had members of my unofficial police force follow all of the members of these tobacconists' staffs and family everywhere. However, it did not take long to identify the individual tobacconist. My informants kept me posted throughout the day. My proprietor's son was followed to the closest newsstand where he avidly waited for the arrival of *The Times* every day. On the day in question, he quickly turned to the agony column, and rushed off as soon as he had read my advertisement. He hurried back to the shop, and made preparations to acquire more infected wool for my special snuff. The rest you know. Once my final destination was identified, we were summoned for the final resolution of the problem."

I looked up at my friend in admiration and asked, "When will we ascertain the identity of 'Little Bo Peep,' the one who is probably the actual murderer?"

"I am afraid that we have a long way to go on that score. The only available witness has been executed. All of the addresses in the special ledger were blinds - a warehouse here, a pub there. Short of exhuming and examining the nasal cavities of all of the thousands of victims of the recent epidemic of influenza, no further steps are available to us. This bears the mark of the unknown master criminal who may always stay beyond my reach. I acknowledge his intelligence and skills. Someday, he will slip up and come within my grasp, but until then, I will have to be satisfied with countering each and every one of his clever thrusts until he finally makes the one fatal error that will undo him."

"Maurice, I cannot wait to write this case up for our annals. It is remarkably singular and demonstrates your skills of deduction to the utmost. The villain sounds like a successor to the now deceased Professor Moriarty. I'm certain that we will encounter him again."

"No, my dear friend and associate, we may never reveal this adventure to the public. Think how such a discovery, if it fell into the hands of a wicked foreign power, would provide a weapon for which we have no available defense. Let us keep this concept of a biological weapon to ourselves and leave it to others to conceive of it on their own. Also, it is essential that, just as the identity of the unseen hand behind these murders remains unknown to me, so must my intervention in his affairs remain hidden from his view. It is likely, however, that he will never use that *modus operandi* again."

Turning my head towards Dr. Verner, I saw that my comrade had finally drifted off into a long awaited and well deserved slumber. The events of the very long day had finally taken their course. Gently, I lay a blanket across my now sleeping friend, and retired to my own bedroom to undergo the depression that overcomes me after the completion of an interesting little problem such as the one that has just been concluded.

[1]Partially based on a story originally published *The Hounds Collection* Volume II, First Edition, April 1997

Dr. Watson and the Adventure of the Pearls of Death – Conclusion

It had been a tiring day for Maurice Verner and his younger cousin Claude. After finally finishing the rush reconstruction job on the 1960s British Racing Green Lotus, they had to drive it to their wealthy client on the beach of Lake Sinclair, Michigan. This was followed by a tedious negotiating session where they finally received the proceeds that they had originally been promised for the work. Then there was the long, tedious drive home in their '67 Mustang back to their secret lair in the warehouses along the Detroit River. Since their wives were displaying their designer gowns at the *nouveau riche* establishment of the co-owner of a newly successful technology firm, the men decided to spend the night in their urban quarters rather than driving all the way back to their suburban homes.. After the men shared their well-earned cold duck cocktails, accompanied by imported cigars, Claude left for his quarters for a bachelor evening with his TV set. Maurice carried his drink into the sequestered Sherlock Holmes sitting room, and resumed his reading of the stories that Dr. Watson had written concerning his adventures with his ancestor, Dr. Maurice Verner.

The episode continued:

The last two weeks had been very trying. Since Mrs. Forrester's husband, the Honorable Mr. Cecil Forrester was still returning by sea from a business trip to Australia, it fell to me to help comfort Mrs. Forrester after the death of her brother-in-law Lord Herbert McFallow, and to practice my skills as an alienist and a friend. The funeral had been delayed one week while the official medical examiner, assisted by Dr. Verner, performed his duties to define the cause of death. It was up to me to arrange the funeral, contact the widower Lord Herbert's few relatives and close friends, and prepare the eulogy. Today, the Sunday two weeks after the death, I was finally able to finish recording my records on my patients from the scribbled notes that I had scribbled during the hectic weeks of respiratory illnesses. Finally finished, I was able to light my pipe, pour a stiff whiskey, and lay down on my sofa. I hoped that I would be able to take a nap before dinner.

However, this was not to be the case. I heard two sets of male footsteps clumping up the stairs. One I recognized as my new friend Dr. Maurice Verner. As the men entered my sitting room, I saw that Maurice was accompanied by the short, well-muscled man I only knew as Mr. Melas, the agent for the British government and the official translator for spies from both sides of the world.

Walking over to the liquor cabinet, Maurice poured a drink for himself and his associate. Lighting a cigar and offering one to Mr. Melas, Maurice looked at me contemplatively and said, "James. I know that you are tired. I have a favor to ask of you, to join us at the government offices after dinner to look at some evidence from the murder of Lord Herbert. Another similar death has taken place, and Mycroft wants me to step in. I think that your expertise would be essential. Pending our discussion of the evidence, we may need to take several trips. I hope that you are willing to join us tomorrow morning for some excursions."

I thought to myself, "Here we go again. Well it will bring me out of my doldrums, at least."

Then aloud I said, "I will of course be very happy to assist. Maybe Mr. Melas would care to join us for dinner."

Mr. Melas responded, "I will be most happy to. As a matter of fact, I would like to invite the pair of you as my guests in the government executive dining room with Mycroft Holmes. I will send a coach to pick you up at 7:00 P.M. I hope this is satisfactory."

My response was to answer in the affirmative since my dinner jacket had been recently cleaned and pressed. As we sat, I got up and refilled the three glasses as we passed another half-hour discussing current events.

After the men left, all thoughts of repose before dinner left my mind as I sorted through the possible activities that might follow from our dinner meeting.

After dressing, Dr. Verner joined me in the sitting room. Almost as soon as he entered, there was a knock on the door.

It was our page boy, Billy, who said, "Gentlemen, there is a carriage waiting for you."

Thus alerted, we donned our top hats and great coats and walked down the stairs to the exit. Billy brushed both of us off and opened the door for our egress. As we trod the sidewalk to the street, we were greeted with an elegant closed coach with a two-horse team. The steeds were coal black and identical. Frosty steam was floating from their opened mouths as they whinnied. While the footman assisted our alighting, I thought to myself, "The government knows how to transport people whose help it needs."

The swift ride took us to government center where two liveried footmen escorted us to an elegant door into a building which I had never before had the privilege of entering. A haughty butler took our hats and coats and directed us up the stairs where we encountered a beautifully appointed dining room. The elaborate furnishings were most impressive. I was so distracted by the upcoming expected events, that I barely recorded the décor. I do recall that the walls were a light blue decorated with horizontal rails of gold, and that the many portraits that covered the walls featured men in military dress dating from the Middle Ages to the current style, and the crystal goblets reflected the brilliantly glowing modern electric lamp above our heads.

Seated in a corner niche was the enormous bulk of Mr. Mycroft Holmes. The important gentleman stood and shook our hands and bade us to be seated on highly stuffed ornate scarlet and gold chairs in the corner. Then Mr. Melas arrived, and he was also cordially welcomed by his old colleague. Mr. Holmes smiled and poured each of us a French aperitif to start our evening.

Then Mr. Holmes greeted us with this, "Welcome to our dining room. After dinner, Mr. Melas and I will have some things to discuss with you concerning the death of Lord Herbert and, in addition, the recent demise of Sir Reginald Armstrong. It would appear that the situation has gone beyond a simple murder. The Home Secretary is concerned that there may be a political component since the two murdered men were working in tandem on important matters of state."

As we ate I barely tasted the food, although I am certain that it featured excellent beef and roasted potatoes – a typical British staple. I was happy that under the circumstance, mutton was not featured. The dry red wine was a perfect accompaniment to the elegantly served victuals.

I was grateful for the time taken to enjoy cigars. That hiatus in alcoholic intake partially allowed my mind to clear for the next event of the evening.

Mr. Holmes left us with a hearty thank you and a promise to contact us for a report of our activities. As we traversed the large dining hall, we departed by a rear door. All elegance was quickly left behind as we entered a utilitarian gray-painted back hall lined by a series of doors. At the end of the gray-painted corridor, we encountered a narrow staircase that was darkly lit by small gas lanterns. Maurice and I slowly followed Melas down the narrow stairs to what appeared to be a subbasement.

Answering Melas' sharp double-knock on the door was the easily recognized deep bass bellow of my former army commander, Colonel Overstreet. I had no problem identifying this tall, thin, clean-shaven man. He had been my superior officer in Afghanistan, and was a man for whom I had great respect and admiration.

"Watson, is it my old comrade?" he called out. "Come in. I've been looking forward to seeing you. And I see that you are accompanied by my old friend Mr. Melas. I trust that the man with you is another doctor, the estimable Dr. Maurice Verner, who cleverly diagnosed the cause of death of Lord Herbert."

After a round of firm handshakes, Colonel Overstreet continued, "I'm hoping that you can bring your expertise to bear on the death of Sir Reginald. His list of symptoms matches those that you reported to the coroner. I've left the windows open so that the cold air could help preserve the bodies."

As we entered the room, I could detect two familiar odors. One was the aroma of deteriorating human flesh, such as that which would be encountered on a battlefield; the other was recognizable as that encountered in a pen of sheep.

Pointing at a body under a sheet on a table near the wall, the Colonel said, "Here he is, Sir Reginald Armstrong. I've laid out all of the tools that were described in your report. In the next room are the appropriate microscopes. Please let me know what else you require. Please allow me to assist you. I miss medical work. My most important instrument the last few years has been a fountain pen. And I'm always ready to learn new techniques."

Mr. Melas distributed warm coats to help stave off the bitter cold. While Drs. Verner and Overstreet began probing the body of Sir Reginald, Melas drew me to another table on which resided a dead sheep, a rifle, and a spent cartridge. Then Melas asked, "What do you think of this evidence collected from the slaughterhouse in which the man who was shearing the sheep was killed? And what is your opinion of the animal?'

I quickly recognized all of the items. I separated the sheep's wool to reveal black growths on its flesh. They were the typical signs of cutaneous anthrax.

I said, "The sheep has anthrax. The rifle is a Martini-Henry that the British soldiers carried in Afghanistan. It fires a .577/450 bottleneck cartridge such as the one laying on the table. Can I assume that this is the weapon that killed the shearer and the projectile that was extracted from his body?"

"Yes," replied Melas. "It was found at the scene of the shooting. The cartridge resided in the heart of the slaughtered man."

I continued, "The rifle and cartridge would suggest that the murderer had served in the British army, and was a regular soldier during my era. Only the British soldiers carried them. The Indian and other non-British regulars were issued old Sniders."

"What about the sheep?" asked Melas.

"I recognized it right away. It is clearly infected with cutaneous anthrax. It is very likely the source of the anthrax bacilli in the contaminated snuff." I answered. "It is a Whiteface from Dartmoor. I think that it is the only locale where they exist in abundance. I would theorize that the man behind the murders resided in Dartmoor. I remember that location very well. I know several people there who could help us identify a man who served in the British army during my era and had access to the local sheep."

"Splendid," replied Melas."How would you like to take a journey there tomorrow?"

I answered, "I would be most happy to help out, as well as renew old acquaintances."

Then I followed Melas to another room. It was nice and toasty warm due to a roaring fire in the hearth. Maurice had preceded us. He was already peering through the low-powered microscope. He looked my way and invited me with a hand gesture to view the field.

"It's a mixture of wool and tobacco, just like that found in Lord Herbert's nose."

After looking through the high-power lens, I saw the deceptively beautiful pearl necklace. In another slide I saw something new. There were rod-shaped bacteria with oval objects within them.

Maurice said, 'This is a spore stain. Colonel Overstreet was able to send for the dye from his research facilities. It's brand new technology. Beautiful, is it not? Gas gangrene bacilli look very similar, but their disease state is quite different and they don't grow aerobically like anthrax bacilli do. Anyway, there is no doubt that Sir Reginald also died from anthrax laden sheep wool mixed with snuff. Tomorrow, we must visit Sir Reginald's abode and look for the sample of snuff."

After our exploration, we thoroughly washed our hands and rinsed them with isopropyl alcohol. Mr. Melas offered to lead us upstairs to the dining room where we would be able to rest and discuss our findings over cigars and aged Cognac. We agreed that we would need to visit Sir Reginald's abode in the morning and then continue our examination with a train ride to Dartmoor.

The following morning, Maurice did not appear to be in a hurry to depart, so we were able to enjoy a full English breakfast of soft boiled eggs, bacon, stewed tomatoes, curry, baked beans, and excellent hot American coffee.

Finally, I queried Maurice about the delay. He responded, "I speculate that there is an argument concerning the case. Does it belong under the purview of the British government or is it a police matter? We are awaiting a warrant to search Sir Reginald's apartment. Ah, I hear Mr. Melas coming up the stairs. The additional footsteps are no doubt those belonging to Inspector Lestrade. It appears that the impasses have been resolved."

As the two government representatives joined us at Billy's motion, we offered them hot coffee and seats by the fire to warm themselves. After completing our refreshment, we followed Mr. Melas into an awaiting government-issue four wheel coach with a pair of beautiful stallions. Off we went until we arrived at the elaborately-carved door of a town house in a nearby suburban estate of Sir Reginald's ancient family.

We departed the coach with the assistance of Sir Reginald's footman and encountered his burly butler, who introduced himself as Barnes, at the magnificent wooden door. He held out a silver circular tray upon which we deposited our calling cards.

He said "Please wait in the front room while I bring your identity cards to Sir Reginald's solicitor, Mr. Dallyrimple, Esquire."

He then ascended the staircase, as the footman helped us remove our hats and overcoats. The return of the butler enabled us to ascend to the private quarters on the first floor.

After carefully returning our documents of identity, Barnes escorted us up the central staircase past family paintings that dated as far back as men in armor. At the landing, we were confronted by a slim goateed man in full business attire, including striped pants, and gray frock coat. His tie and watch fob indicated that he was a first-honor graduate of King's College. After looking us over, he seemed assured of our professional status and our estate as gentlemen and lowered his nose so that his eyes met ours.

In a thin whiny voice he said, "May I see your warrant to search the premises?"

As Lestrade handed the official papers over, the lawyer said, "It would appear that you have arrived late. Someone has broken into Sir Reginald's apartment and ransacked it. Whatever is of importance to you gentlemen is, no doubt, unavailable."

Following the solicitor through the various rooms, we noticed that everything was littered about. All of the furniture had been toppled over. The artwork had been removed from the wall and torn open. The cushions on the chairs and bedding had been torn asunder, and stuffing was abundant everywhere. Lestrade shrugged his shoulders and turned to leave. I began to follow, but Maurice and Melas both grabbed my arm and retarded my exit.

Maurice said, "Let's not give up too soon. Whatever the searcher hoped to find may have been secreted so well that only an intelligent evaluation would find the location of the important item. Something very secret was hidden here."

Emulating our master Sherlock Holmes, we did a more thorough investigation. We removed the rug and looked for loose floor boards. We banged on the wall searching for hollow places. Then it hit me. I removed the telephone from its stand and dismantled it. Inside the receiver was a circular horn-like device. Using my knife, I removed the horn to reveal a piece of paper stuffed under it. Surrounded by my associates, I unrolled the paper and then unfolded it on my knee. It was titled, 'Ballarat Gold Shares Cooperative.' There was a list of six names, of which I recognized three; Sir Reginald Armstrong, Lord Herbert McFallow, Mr. Cecil Forrester. I was also surprised to see Mr. James Mortimer, and Sir Henry Baskerville. Another, unknown to me, was Mr. Silas Grant. It was notarized and bore the signature of Mr. Dallyrimple, Esq. No doubt; the clues will take us to Dartmoor, the home of the latter men as well as the source of the sheep used in the contamination of the deadly snuff. Hopefully, both the physician, Mr. Mortimer, and the Baronet, Sir Henry, had not been infected. Our communication with Mr. Forrester would have to await the culmination of his ocean voyage from

Australia. I looked at the Bradshaw to find the fastest train to take us to Dartmoor. Melas courteously invited Lestrade to join us in our venture. A note handed to Sir Reginald's buttons sent a telegram with which we acquired a suite of rooms at the local hostelry in Coombs Tracey.

Before leaving, I asked and received all of the snuff containers in Sir Reginald's possession, and warned the solicitor of the vile contents that may lead to death by anthrax. He handed me six green circular containers of snuff from the same tobacconist who had apparently supplied Lord Herbert.

The train ride through Devonshire was uneventful. At every stop, Maurice requested the local newspapers. He quickly scanned the contents and then stuffed the finished item under the seat. Finally, coming to our last stop, Maurice reviewed the journal, smiled, and retained the weekly publication from Coombs Tracy.

He said, "As I expected, there was an anthrax epidemic amongst some of the Dartmoor sheep. We will need to visit the owner of the farm, a Silas Grant. The good news is that none of the remaining men on the list from the 'Ballarat Gold Shares Cooperative,' whatever that is, has been killed. That is fortunate. Our first job will be to thoroughly check their domiciles for infected snuff, medically examine them, and interview them.

After departing the train, a wagonet was located to take us and our luggage to the nice, clean hostelry. Two double-bedded sleeping rooms, a bath, and a bright sitting room were awaiting us. After depositing our luggage, we went down the stairs to look for lunch. After dining on excellent cod sandwiches and local ale in a well appointed and clean restaurant, we decided to go back to freshen up and then plan a strategy to get to the bottom of the mystery.

The first order of business was to warn James Mortimer, Silas Grant, and Sir Henry of the danger. Should they use the snuff, it would mean certain death. As the acknowledged leader of our group, Maurice had taken on the role that was once assumed by Sherlock Holmes. Lestrade was assigned to contact the local police and, with their assistance, inform Sir Henry, Mr. Grant, and James Mortimer of the danger, and seek out anyone else who might have received the snuff, since we didn't yet know if the Cooperative members were the only targets of the murderer. Melas, with the assistance of other agents that he had called to the scene, used their guile to find out what secret activities might point to the problem to help us with its resolution. None of the local inhabitants seemed aware of the events that we were exploring.

Maurice and I went to the sheep farm to find out the involvement of the staff. After the departure of our co-investigators, Maurice and I found a local livery stable and rented the service of two excellent stallions for the visit to the sheep farm. Following the directions of the manager of the stable, we quickly exited the tiny town. The rugged dirt road suited our conveyances, and the odor of the sheep farm and the baying of the sheep hounds easily guided us to our destination. As we dismounted, a young man in rough, dirty, rural attire approached us and told us that were not welcome. There had been some sheep missing, and the governor didn't brook the presence of strangers.

The man's attitude changed when Maurice held out a five-pound note and said, "We mean no harm. We want to be your friends. Could you get your employer for us? We want to buy some sheep for the market in London."

The man replied, "Funny that you should say that. Our boss told us that he is going to London, and that if anyone wants to see him he will be at the docks waiting for the ship 'Rock of Gibraltar.' The Harbormaster will know where he is staying."

Maurice replied, "Did he say when the ship will arrive?"

"The boss said in two weeks from tomorrow. Meanwhile he is on other business."

"One other question," said Maurice, holding out the currency, "Have you lost any sheep to anthrax?"

"Yes," replied the worker." We lost two animals. The sick ones were taken away with the master. He wanted to bury them very deeply in an isolated part of the farm."

"A final question, did Mr. Grant receive a supply of snuff?"

"Not that I recall," answered the man, with a sign of irritation in his voice.

"Thank you for your kind help," said Maurice, handing over the money. Giving the man his card, Maurice said, in parting. "Please tell your governor to contact us when he returns. We will be in London at our medical office. We hope that he has not caught this disease. We would like to help him if we could. Tell him not to use the snuff in a green box if it arrives."

As we mounted and slowly rode away, Maurice turned to me and said, "The Rock of Gibraltar is the finest ship traveling from Adelaide. Didn't Mrs. Forrester say that her husband would be arriving from Australia? And that is the finest steamship in the fleet with luxurious suites as befits a man such as Mr. Forrester. And recall that the secret cabal has a Ballarat connection. I wonder if gold mining is involved as implied in one of your stories concerning Sherlock Holmes' first case."

After returning to the inn, we met for some liquid refreshment. We greeted Lestrade and informed him of what we had learned. He said that he would telegraph the London police to safeguard Mr. Forrester. Then, Lestrade had a note for us from Sir Henry scribbled on very expensive paper bearing a Canadian water mark. The note read:

My Dear Dr. Watson,

Thank you for the warning. I did receive some snuff last week. Fortunately, I didn't use it since I consider it a filthy habit.

I look forward to seeing you and meeting your friend. Would you both do the honor of joining Mortimer and me for dinner in Baskerville Hall? Silas Grant has left for business in London, so he won't be able to join us. Since I'm a basically a Canadian farmer, we will have beer and a bar-b-q. Come as you are. We rarely dress for dinner. I have a chuck wagon cook who used to join me on cattle drives in my youth. Please let me know and I can send a wagon for you. After dinner, we can discuss recent events in town. I'm very curious about how murder and infected snuff are associated."

Naturally, both Maurice and I assented to the invitation. I had never been invited to a cowboy event before. Also, I was curious about what changes had been made in the gloomy hall. Meanwhile, Lestrade and Melas decided to eat in the local pub and scout out gossip about the sheep farm, epidemic of anthrax, and any other events of note.

Unlike past experiences, when Baskerville Hall was wreathed in fog and eerie darkness, my eyes were now dazzled by all of the brilliant electric lamps that illuminated the tree alley towards the main gate. What had once been the frightening death run for Sir Charles was now a clear welcoming path. Another thing that struck my senses was the pounding of the pistons and whistle of steam as the generator powered enormous quantities of electric current throughout the house and its grounds. As we entered the main hall at the invitation of the large ruddy butler, I noticed that the previously gloomy staircase to the upper floors was also bright and welcoming. I especially noted the beautiful artwork, including the smirking portrait of Sir Hugo, the ancient family villain.

As Sir Henry descended the stairs arm in arm with what had to be his beautiful wife, I could easily see that a new heir to the estate was in the process of gestation. I silently hoped that the child would be blessed with a long and happy life with its parents.

Sir Henry, stepping into the hall, extended a warm smile and handshake welcoming Maurice and me into his abode. His wife, named Adele, who also had her own title of Dame Adele, approached us in a very friendly and cordial manner. The couple was attired in appropriate dress for the occasion with homespun trousers and shirts. Their feet were shod with cowboy boots. I was informed that Adele was also a native of Canada. Fittingly, she wore a cowboy hat and yellow braids hung down her back. Sir Henry had a thin mustache similar to that sported by actors in English melodramas. However, his manner was open and his accent clearly marked him as a Canadian. As is their tradition, we quickly began to call one another by our first names.

I was grateful for their thoughtfulness. I felt perfectly comfortable and at home in my traveling tweeds. Our interactions reminded me of those I encountered during my brief stay in Baltimore, attending special neuroscience courses at Johns Hopkins Medical School.

As we traversed the house, I began to smell the delicious odor of Canadian bar-b-q. The rear forest had been cleared into a vast field. The trees had been removed and had been reduced into prodigious piles of firewood for the Edison generator and the cooking fire. The sky was cheery and brightened by the full moon and the enormous lights.

Maurice and I were invited to join the couple at a log table with simple wooden chairs. In the North American tradition, ice cold glasses were filled with frothy frigid

Canadian ale. A pair of casually-dressed waiters placed huge platters on the table, and passed piles of pork ribs, baked beans, and fried green tomatoes in front of us. Then, they brought bowls of fresh pickles and raw vegetables to complete the offerings. As the food and beverages became depleted, they were immediately replaced by fresh supplies. The conversation was friendly and informative, but no business was discussed. We learned that Mr. and Mrs. Stapleton's house was now rented to a nice American couple who wanted to study our Neolithic ancestors. There was a new young rector at the church who attracted the attention of the local ladies. And, as usual, there was some humorous discussion of various trespass cases being circulated.

Apparently, Sir Henry was doing very well. As an experienced farmer with a large holding in Canada as well, he was very adept at land management. Everything was going as planned except for a few cases of anthrax among the sheep on the land that he rented to Mr. Silas Grant. The last name piqued my interest, and Maurice and I nodded to one another as soon as we heard it.

We were then joined by Mr. Mortimer and his wife, Elizabeth, who was another physician from London. They were both in their mid-forties and dressed in the casual style expected of an English couple at a picnic: he in tweeds and she in a white petticoat. They had been called away at the last minute to deliver a baby. They quickly devoured the food put before them, and joined the conversation. Fortunately, Mortimer avoided his topic of head size and shape.

As the evening wore on, the chill air forced the participants into the beautifully appointed mansion. It was brightly lit. The furnishings, although spotless and clean, hearkened back to an earlier era of opulence. In the more British surroundings, they were offered a variety of after dinner drinks and the men, after getting permission from the females, lighted cigars. Accordingly, Dame Adele removed a slim cigarette from a silver holder on the table at their feet. Sir Henry used a large silver lighter to set it alight.

As we relaxed, discussion took a very friendly tone. The ladies began to bemoan the fact that they had not received any mail for a few days. Apparently, the postmistress had been assaulted and all of the mail stolen. Everyone had been shocked by the occurrence in what was normally a quiet town. Mr. Mortimer stated that the post mistress' injuries were not severe, but she was unable to identify her two male attackers who wore bandanas tied over their faces. Then the discussion went to other matters. Maurice and I avoided any discussion of our murder investigation. We quietly digested all of the information that came our way.

Eventually, Maurice and I turned the conversation to subtleties regarding football, cricket, and rugby. As expected, the ladies' eyes glazed over and they excused themselves to "freshen up." Having achieved our goal, Maurice and I were now able to inquire about the secret business of the 'Ballarat Gold Shares Cooperative.'

Maurice was very blunt in his opening statement; "We are here to prevent additional murders associated with the 'Ballarat Gold Shares Cooperative'."

After several minutes of hesitation, Sir Henry was the first to comment. He stated, heatedly, "What are you talking about? There is no such organization."

Maurice replied, as he removed the folded document from his left hand pants pocket, "This is why we warned you about infected snuff and told you to give it to us. At first, we determined that the death of Lord Herbert McFallow was caused by using snuff mixed with wool from a sheep. When we investigated the source of the anthrax-infected wool, we were about to apprehend the person who was clipping the wool in a slaughterhouse. Unfortunately, he was shot with a military rifle. The killer escaped. We traced the sheep to your vicinity. It was a white-faced Dartmoor. Later, we were invited to explore the mysterious death of Sir Reginald Armstrong. When we searched his home, we found this document very well hidden in his office telephone. In fact, someone else had previously broken into his home and searched it thoroughly, probably without success. We deduced that this mysterious document was somehow associated with the deaths. We feared that that similarly labeled snuff had been sent to you. We assumed that the document was the source of the killings. Now, gentlemen, it is time to openly discuss this document with us. We promise to maintain your confidence."

"OK" reticently replied Mr. Mortimer, "We purchased shares of a gold mine that is located in Ballarat, Australia. We wanted to keep it secret so that no one else would share our income, should the project come to fruition. We expect to hear soon from Mr. Cecil Forrester, who is now returning from Australia on the ship 'Rock of Gibraltar' as you indicated. We expect mail very soon regarding our fortune."

"Very well." I responded. "Your secret is safe with us. We are only interested in ending the murders. There are now only two men at risk: Mr. Forrester and Mr. Grant. Mr. Forrester may become endangered when he arrives in London. We were unable to determine if Mr. Grant received snuff. We will try to find him in London to find out. We are assisting highly placed government officials under an order of state security. They are not aware of the financial connection between you gentlemen, and it's none of their business. It appears that some of the men are working together on a diplomatic project. However, we do have some clues to follow. Whom do you know that has Whiteface Dartmoor Sheep, and has been troubled with anthrax?"

Sir Henry replied, "All of us farmers have anthrax problems. It is a contagion ubiquitous in the environment. The only way to handle it is to deeply bury any infected animals."

Maurice then continued, "Whom do you know that has such sheep that were infected with anthrax, and served in the British army?"

Mr. Mortimer inquired, "How is that appropriate?"

I responded, "The killer of the sheep shearer left behind his rifle in his haste to elude us. He probably didn't want to be seen running through the streets of London with an army rifle."

Mortimer continued, "What brand of rifle was it? I know everyone's weapons."

I replied, "The rifle was a Martini-Henry rifle, similar to the ones that the British troops used in Afghanistan. The shell that was extracted from the slain man was the typical .577/450 cartridge. The shot from the distance of over 300 feet into the man's heart indicated that the shooter was a marksman. Does anyone come to mind?"

"The only man who fills all of the criteria is Silas Grant. He has been troubled with anthrax in his sheep which are Whiteface Dartmoor, and has lost considerable sums of money. Also, he is a sniper who served in the army in Afghanistan. He is a member of our consortium and could reap a fortune by buying shares at low prices from our heirs, should we die before they can be redeemed. But, he is a very honorable man. The last we knew, he left for London to await Cecil Forrester."

Looking at our watches, Maurice and I nodded to one another as Maurice said, "Gentlemen, you have given us some information to chew on. If you think of anything else, please contact me. Here is our address, please let us know if you see Mr. Grant and please warn him about the snuff," he concluded, handing Mortimer and Sir Henry our cards. "We will look for him in London and meet Mr., Forrester when his ship arrives."

I ended the evening with, "Please give my regards to your lovely wives. Thank you very much for a most enjoyable evening of Canadian delicacies and for making us feel at home."

We shook hands, sought our coach, and departed for our rooms in town. However, on the way, we requested that we be dropped off at the popular pub, the *Giant Hound*. There we encountered our colleagues Melas and Lestrade to see whatever information they dug up, drawing them away from the boisterous crowd of workers, whose tongues they had no doubt loosened by free alcohol. Unlike the more staid business men, this group was more likely to discuss the inner workings of town from the street level point of view.

As we shook hands, Lestrade said, "I have some interesting news for you. Last week, the post office was ransacked after the postmistress was assaulted. No mail has been delivered in town for three days. I don't think the gentry would even have known about that. I got more details than I wanted from the constable, whose drinks we shared. Also, the farm workers said that Silas Grant disappeared immediately after that event."

As we sipped our last beverage of the late evening, we agreed that we had plowed the field sufficiently to justify a return trip to London in the afternoon. We had earned a large breakfast at Imperial expense the following morning.

Taking the long train ride back to the Baker Street Station, we discussed the future of transportation. Always advanced in his understanding of science, Maurice championed the use of steam propelled vehicles to replace horse-drawn coaches. The application of hot steam would have the advantage of providing heated cabins, such as those available on the modern steam ships. Further, the smell of London would be enhanced by the lack of horse droppings on the streets. I somewhat agreed, and wondered how Holmes would have reacted. Lestrade was adamantly opposed to such new-fangled ideas, and Melas remarked that attempts were being made in Germany to adopt the burning of liquid petrol to power the wheels of vessels.

I awoke in late morning after a well deserved rest. My head spun with a mixture of the power of steam and the mystery of our venture. However, unused to all of the alcoholic beverages we had consumed, my head was pounding and I had very little appetite. My breakfast consisted only of toast, butter, and orange marmalade washed down with voluminous quantities of strong black coffee. Maurice's handwritten note left on the table informed me that he had already dined and was off to the docks to obtain information on shipping schedules from Australia. He suggested that we meet for lunch at a nice seafood restaurant near the port to discuss our next activities. He asked me to visit Mrs. Forrester to get her husband's travel schedule. Also, I needed to see how her husband and Mr. Silas Grant were connected.

Over lunch on fish stew and muffins, we conversed on the status of our investigation. Maurice said, "So far we have saved the lives of Sir Henry Baskerville and Mr. James Mortimer. Of course, the villain of this piece might not be aware of our intervention. We will need to keep it secret."

I replied, "Yes, about the other men on the list of investors, Lord Herbert McFallow and Sir Reginald Armstrong were murdered by anthrax laced snuff. Mr. Forrester is on a voyage home from Australia investigating their investment. That leaves Mr. Silas Grant. Could he have been the one who robbed the post office and then disappeared? Did he possibly steal the mail sent by Mr. Forrester they all awaited before deciding to sell or retain their shares? Mrs. Forrester told me that her husband and Silas Grant had just met and were not friends."

In response, Maurice said, "I guess we will need to find out when Mr. Forrester's ship, the steamship 'Rock of Gibraltar' will disembark. We should meet him at the ship as soon as it arrives. We need to protect him and keep him from using the dangerous snuff. I'll discuss that with Melas and Lestrade after we consult with the shipping office of the Southampton Line. Meanwhile, we can investigate the arrival of the mail from Australia on the faster clipper ship 'City of Adelaide.' If Mr. Forrester sent word before he left Australia that would be the ship to carry it. Would someone try to intercept it at the shipping office?"

"In the meantime," I said, "We can impose on the government agencies to look for Mr. Silas Grant so that we can question him and determine his actions.

The day after our arrival in London, we decided to visit the shipping lines. We had plenty of time on our hands. The nice sunny weather and a cold clear day, conspired against the transmission of infectious disease. Apparently the resistance of potential patients was enhanced by their joyful dispositions. We took a Hansom cab down to the docks where we found a clean restaurant with food worthy of our palettes. We then trolled to the elegant offices of the Southampton Line, where the 'Rock of Gibraltar' from Adelaide was expected to dock in five days. All reports from passing ships suggested the veracity of the schedule. So we knew that in five days, Mr. Forrester might need our intervention. The diminution of clipper ships as a source of passenger travel had caused a deterioration of the amenities at the Clipper Ship London Terminal. However, after we finally located an agent, we were informed that the mail from the 'City of Adelaide' had all been picked up. They noted that there had been several pieces destined for the Dartmoor region, and that none were removed short of their destination. The agent was adamant at the suggestion that private parties could have short-circuited the official handling of the mail.

Later that afternoon, Maurice went to the government center and Scotland Yard to arrange for their services in locating Mr. Silas Grant. The next three days went as usual. A return to wet and chilly climate had the anticipated effect of infectious disease. Maurice and I were very busy visiting patients in their homes, work, and hospital. When we came back to our surgeries to resupply, there were always several more patients awaiting us. Thus, it was not until late in the evening when Maurice, who had just arrived, was waiting with Messer's Melas and Lestrade with urgent need of our services. A man had been found dead in a rented room near the shipping offices. The man was nude and had no identification. However, strewn near his body were found several letters addressed to names familiar to us from the list of the gold mine investors.

Mr. Lestrade had already interviewed the manager of the rooming house, a modestly respectable site for people awaiting the arrival of ships prior to their voyage. According to Lestrade, the dead man had been suffering from difficulty breathing most of the day. In his hand was clutched the green round container of the dangerous snuff that served as the centerpiece of our adventure.

'Who is the man?" asked Mr. Melas.

Mr. Lestrade repeated this query, and I was also unable to respond with certainty, although I had my suspicion that it was Silas Grant.

Maurice replied, "This is Mr. Silas Grant. It looks as if he was also a target for murder, rather than a perpetrator. It is unlikely that he would purposely poison himself in such a painful manner."

"How the devil do you know who he is?" asked the incredulous Lestrade. "You are not Sherlock Holmes."

"It is merely a matter of obtaining evidence and using observation."

Then Maurice pulled a folded newspaper from the voluminous pocket in his coat where he secreted many of his medical needs. He said, "Here is a report on the anthrax epidemic in Whiteface Dartmoor sheep. Mr. Grant's photograph has been provided for our edification."

Mr. Melas summed up our supposition, "Now we can agree that Silas Grant was not the villain who provided anthrax to his partners. None of them are left. But someone with evil intent is no doubt awaiting the return of Mr. Forrester; someone who is probably not aware that two of the partners survived due to your intervention. The letters were probably strewn about to cast suspicion on an unidentifiable victim."

Lestrade nodded, "I agree. We must now wait for Mr. Forrester to arrive, and prevent his death. Dr. Watson and Dr. Verner, you have done a commendable service so far. Please join us at the arrival of the 'Rock of Gibraltar' when it docks.

My remaining days were filled with eagerness. We would have the opportunity to unmask the evil person who has so far killed four people for material gain. And he wasn't certain that it would even be financially beneficial to him. He put so little value on human life. Finally the time arrived. Maurice and I made sure that we loaded our revolvers and pocketed them. We also picked up our stoutest sticks and sharpest knives. We had a light lunch, and left our quarters to meet the coach provided by the British Government. I felt very special to be riding in that conveyance with the British insignia upon it.

As we walked up the gangplank, we were pleased to see that several constables were blocking the exit of disembarking passengers. In the distant line, I could see the rather tall, well-dressed figure of Mr. Forrester. A slim, short man in a steward's uniform was presenting him with a thank-you package. Mr. Melas leaped past the waiting crowd, shoving many irate passengers aside. He grabbed the arms of the steward, forcing him to drop the presents.

Simultaneously, the steward and Mr. Forrester yelled, "Stop, thief! We are being robbed."

By the time that the ship's security patrol responded from the entry of the gangplank, Mr. Lestrade and several uniformed constables came to Melas' rescue. Maurice and I took Mr. Forrester's arms, and turning him we showed him that we were friends. As he looked at me, I said, "Don't use the snuff in that package. It is poisoned with anthrax and has already taken the life of Lord Herbert, Sir Reginald, and Silas Grant. It has to do with your gold shares. I hope their value justifies the taking of three lives!"

Demonstrating his concern for his fellow investors' lives, Mr. Forrester asked, "How about Sir Henry and Mr. Mortimer?"

I replied, "With the help of Mr. Melas and Mr. Lestrade," I said, pointing their way, "we were able to warn your friends and remove any leftover packages of the snuff from the provider."

Then Lestrade brought the steward facing Maurice and me. I realized right away who it was. He was the only man left who had complete knowledge of the Ballarat Gold group. Also, since my training in disguises with Sherlock Holmes, I easily discerned the fake beard. Upon removing it, I exposed the face of the solicitor, Mr. Dallyrimple that I had confronted previously.

The man's imperious attitude quickly vanished. His face melted into a beet-red visage filled with anger and embarrassment. As the tears rolled down his blushing cheeks he cried out in a whiny voice, "How could this have happened? It was a perfect plan. But you have no evidence. This won't stand up in the police court!"

Lestrade bowed to Melas and, leading the official police force away, stated "I now turn your fate over to the mercy of officers of the crown. The people whose deaths you caused are high ranking in the Queen's government. You will no doubt become a guest of the British Government under less than affable circumstance.

With a wave of his hand, Mr. Melas summoned two very burly uniformed military men who roughly led the solicitor away. Mr. Melas formally shook my hand and that of Maurice. He said that Mr. Mycroft would want to see us later in the week to formally present us with certificates of merit.

Maurice and I were gratified that we were able to bring this case to a resolution. The receipts of checks totaling 5000 pounds from our companions in Dartmoor were also welcome recompense for our labors. The 'Ballarat Gold Shares Cooperative' was no doubt a very successful enterprise.

Drs. Verner and Watson: The Tetanus Epidemic

The solitude of my sitting room was interrupted by a loud sharp high baritone voice calling my name from the bottom of the steps leading to the door of the quarters I shared with Sherlock Holmes. It was very unusual. Most visitors asked for my colleague. What was even more stunning was the fact that Mr. Holmes left his normal tripartite route from home to his government office to the Diogenes Club. I immediately assumed that our nation must be on the brink of war or some other catastrophe. However, Mr. Mycroft Holmes clearly called out "Dr. Watson, I need your services immediately."

The senior Mr. Holmes' ponderous steps caused the stairs to squeak due to his immense weight. However, he seemed to be in better physical shape that I supposed, since he had reached my doorway in a brief time.

I quickly got to my feet, reluctantly laying *The British Medical Journal* on the table next to my arm chair. The huge Mr. Holmes strode into the center of my sitting room. After shaking hands with my unexpected visitor, I invited him to sit across from me, and offered him a cigar and a whiskey and soda.

As usual, Mr. Holmes required a period of rest after such exertion. He carefully and methodically lighted his cigar and took a healthy drink from the glass. His broad, clean shaven face was, as usual, very serious in mien. Then, in his studied officious manner he said, "There is an emergency. There is an epidemic of tetanus that has come to the attention of the highest medical authorities in the Kingdom. So far, three healthy men have succumbed to this illness, and another is just experiencing the beginning of lockjaw."

In my surprise I queried, "How could there be an epidemic of tetanus? It is not a contagious disease. Cases are usually traced back to an animal bite or a wound with a dirty object. How do you know that it is not some other contagion?"

Mr. Holmes countered, "No evidence exists for the disease to be associated with any normal source of infection. The three dead bodies and the ill person are in the care of your friend Dr. Maurice Verner. He is now awaiting us in his bacteriology laboratory. Maurice has performed bacteriological analysis. He is certain of the etiology of the infection. Although he is quite capable of diagnosing this disorder, he feels that someone with your experience, having worked so closely with my brother, might help him define the source of this infection. The circumstances might point to a case of multiple murders, but they are far from random. All of the victims are clearly Chinese. The bodies were nude and devoid of identification. If the public learned of these events, they would be frightened and respond as they did in the 'Jack the Ripper' activities. In addition, the Chinese residents of London would be very upset. They would, no doubt, worry about a nationalistic motive. I would ask Sherlock to assist us, but he is currently employed in a secret case in Serbia involving poisoned herring. You and my cousin Maurice have been very instrumental in solving medical issues. I trust that you will succeed again."

Finishing our beverages more quickly than we would have liked, I stood up and put on a light waistcoat. We trod down the 17 stairs from my abode and emerged to a beautiful sunny day in Baker Street. It was pleasant late spring. It was an interruption in the rainy season and before the summer heat overtakes London.

We rode in Mr. Holmes' very comfortable and ornate four-wheeler. Arriving at Maurice's medical building, Mr. Holmes said, "I will leave you to your medical affairs as I return to affairs of state." He drove away, leaving me in front of the quarters that Maurice and I had once shared, and that he had recently purchased.

I climbed the steps to Maurice's bacteriology laboratory and clinic on the second level of his medical suite. Unlike the decorated ground floor and habitation on the first floor,, there was no ornamentation on the walls. The facility had been stripped of wall paper and any other ornamentation, making it a clearly scientific venue. As I entered, I saw that Maurice was perusing the nude body of a very well-built young man. The man was athletic but somewhat shorter than us.

Maurice's hawk like visage was set in the particularly deep concentration that he assumed while in the middle of his experimentation. As he loomed his great height over the steel table bearing the subject of his investigation, his penetrating gray eyes were focused on the dying man upon whom he was working. His sharply defined face, bearing a strong resemblance to his cousin, Sherlock Holmes, was set and virtually unmoving. Maurice briefly acknowledged my presence with a small nod and returned his attention to his task.

I noted that the face of the victim had the features and pigmentation of an East Asian man. His visage was frozen into a *rhisus sardonicus*, as if he had been poisoned with strychnine. His nude light yellowish tan-skinned body had the hall marks of a well conditioned athlete. I pitied the poor man as I watched him undergo violent convulsions. He clenched his jaw in a most unnatural fashion and then became immobilized in death. Peering over the victim, I noted that it was mottled with pussy sores along his sternum. This indicated multiple possible points of infectious introduction. My experience on the battlefield indicated that tetanus was the likely cause of his demise. However, there is usually only one wound, such as a bullet, or contamination of an open wound with soil. Bacteriological evidence was required to confirm my tentative diagnosis.

Maurice sampled each of the lesions with heat-sterilized wire needles. He prepared a microscopic slide from each.

He turned to me and said, "After these slides dry, you can help me Gram-stain them. I'm certain that I know what we will find. Please hand me these mice from the cage next to your elbow. I suspect that these are bacteria that do not tolerate oxygen, and do not grow in typical culture medium. If they appear otherwise, I can always propagate them in culture for further definition."

Setting the slides aside, he used hypodermic needles to extract pus from each of the sores and injected a white mouse intravenously with a specimen from each. Each of the animals quickly experienced tetanic convulsions and died. Setting aside these samples and the experimental animals, Maurice bathed his hands with isopropanol and washed them thoroughly with lye soap and water, and ordered me to do the same. After drying his hands, my medical colleague smiled and shook hands with me, and beckoned me to descend the stairs to more comfortable chambers. Later, refreshed with whiskey, we were prepared to discuss Maurice's findings.

After our brief rest, we again ascended the stairs to the laboratory. Donning gloves, we both gently dried the slides over a Bunsen flame and subjected them to traditional Gram stain procedure. Observing the images in the high power microscopic lens, assisted with oil of immersion, we confirmed the presence of bluish-violet Gram-positive rod-shaped bacteria. None had taken up the red counter stain of safranine. Some cells displayed the circular club-shaped attachments on their ends characteristic of bacterial spores. They microbes clearly tetanus bacilli. The only bacteriological mystery was the source of the infection and the intent of the perpetrator.

We again retreated down to Maurice's comfortable sitting room to enjoy the mandatory whiskey and cigars, and to discuss our findings. As we sat in conversation, we were joined by Maurice's lovely blonde-haired wife Jeanine. The tall French woman was carrying several large sheets of paper. Before sitting between us in one of the four side chairs, she assembled the drawings side-by-side on the large rectangular table in the center of our furniture arrangement. They were sketches of the abdomens of the four victims. Most noteworthy was the fact that the images were virtually identical. The lesions were all arrayed in a symmetrical order down the center of the men's abdomens in double rows.

These were clearly the result of planned, ritual murder. But who was devious enough to organize this event, and why was it done? If ever we needed the presence of Sherlock Holmes, this was it. And, as fate would have it, Sherlock Holmes strode into our view with our boy in buttons, Billy, trailing in his wake. Seeing the images laid out on the table, Holmes quickly stated, "This has some very interesting clues. I would be very happy to assist you, if you so desired. I have several hours available before I venture to the Serbian legation."

Both Maurice and I exclaimed loudly in unison, "Of course. We need your help!"

Then, in the high pitched voice that he used when organizing an investigation, Mr. Holmes said, "Let us examine the deceased firsthand. The sketches, done by the hands of Maurice's very talented artist wife, are of great use. However, I must examine the bodies for myself. Then I will need to look at the site from which the remains were extracted, and see if there were any witnesses to the obvious abduction."

Following Sherlock Holmes rapid pace, we ran up the two levels to Maurice's bacteriological research station. Maurice escorted us into his large 400 square foot, very modern, refrigerated room. The atmosphere was nauseating. It contained a mixture of crepitating bodies and a slight odor of the refrigerant, ammonia. In addition to the body that we had recently sampled were three others of very similar racial appearances. As we stood aside in awe, we watched as Holmes bent his wiry gaunt frame over each of the victims in turn. He felt and examined with his huge hand lens every inch of their bodies on both superior and posterior surfaces. He looked deeply into their eyes and mouths, sniffing at their oral cavities for tell-tale signs of intoxication.

Then Holmes led us out of the refrigerated unit into the warmth of the outer laboratory. Putting on fresh gloves, he carefully examined the dead mice with his hand lens and viewed the microscopic slides.

His first pronouncement to Maurice was, "Telephone our friend Percy Phelps. He owes us a big favor. Have him arrange for Her Majesty's government to take control of the bodies for a case under government jurisdiction. Do not inform the local authorities or tell anyone else of this situation. After that, I have a job for Maurice."

Turning to his cousin, Holmes said, "Maurice, please go to the Chinese quarter and bring back Dr. Huang Lee. We will need his expertise in the ancient Chinese art of acupuncture. He will be able to tell you which of the various practitioners of this medical procedure use this style. Then, ask Dr. Huang if there are any special athletic events involving gentlemen of his heritage. Please retain him so that I may question him on my return later tonight. He enjoys Cuban cigars and gin."

Maurice turned to his cousin and queried, "How do you know that the infection was induced by acupuncture and that these men are athletes?"

Holmes smiled slightly, happy that his cousin was interested in the deductive process. He responded, "On my recent journey to Asia during my absence from Europe, I was able to study many Chinese medical practices, and I am certain that the microbe was introduced by that procedure. As to the men's identity as athletes, a quick look at their knees and palms would indicate rough use. I would guess that these men are rugby players. They are built similarly and are well muscled. Unlike football players, there is no evidence that they use their heads to impact the ball. Perhaps if we go to the area that the victims were extracted from, we would get some idea of their identity. They were found nude, with no source of identification. I understand that the Chinese quarter of London would be good starting point. Fortunately, I have acquired the ability to speak both Mandarin and Cantonese. Watson, would you accompany me?"

I quickly responded in the affirmative and we set out running down the stairs to an awaiting Hansom cab. Wishing to be involved in the action, Billy had preceded us into the vehicle.

Holmes said, "Billy, I may have special need of your knowledge of the darker side of life. Please let me know if you have any ideas. I think I may have a glimmer of a motive for these murders."

Following Holmes' instructions, our carriage took us to a part of London to which I have never ventured. He indicated that the bodies had been retrieved from an alley in that vicinity. There were no street lights. Night had fallen and it was somewhat dark, except for the garishly lighted restaurants and the few store windows displaying pharmaceutical paraphernalia with labels in the Chinese fashion.

Following in Holmes wake, I marveled at his command of the Chinese dialects as he questioned various individuals up and down both sides of the street. However, it was obvious that no useful information was forthcoming.

As we turned the corner and went around the block, we entered a very different neighborhood. It was seedy and littered with garbage. There was a plethora of bars in which poorly dressed men drank mugs of beer, talked loudly, and played darts.

Pointing to the largest door front of a closed darkened facility, Billy said, "I know this location. I've only seen it during the day. It is a well known betting parlor."

As we illuminated the window with modern electric torches, we noted a large display sign therein advertising a picture of a rugby match between Chinese and British athletes.

Billy piped in his boy soprano, "Ain't these like the blokes that I helped carry into Dr. Verner's laboratory?"

Holmes added, "According to my interpretation of the Chinese script, this is a very important match. The betting odds are in favor of the visiting Chinese from Hong Kong. I smell a rat. We may need to visit this locale and take the proprietors into custody. I will communicate this with Mr. Phelps who, as you know, is an agent of the British government. However, it is time for me to leave you. I will be back to Dr. Verner's quarters this evening to interview Dr. Huang Lee.

Our work done for the evening, Billy and I took a Hansom cab back to our former abode. When the page boy and I arrived at my prior medical clinic, now occupied by Dr. Maurice Verner, we noted that Dr. Huang was already there.

After convivial introductions and congenial greetings between me and my Chinese medical colleague, we shared alcoholic beverages and cigars. After our conversation commenced, I realized that I had encountered Dr. Huang several years before when we were both sitting for our doctoral exams and awaiting our thesis defense. At the time, the then Mr. Huang appeared as any other Chinese of the time, except that he was very tall. He had worn a brightly colored robe and his feet were encased in soft soled shoes. Now, he was in every aspect the image of a successful British Doctor of Medicine from his frock coat, Albert chain, and highly polished shoes. He spoke with a clipped accent that would have pleased an English master from Oxford or Cambridge. I would never have recognized him had I passed by him in the street.

Billy left to perform his other activities.

Jeanine joined us to display her drawings of the deceased men and their lesions.

The Chinese doctor took one look at the sketches and stated, following a disdainful snort, "This not the work of a trained Chinese medical practitioner. We place great emphasis on the art of acupuncture, and the precise location of the nerves that we are activating. Recently, several British-born interlopers have attempted to emulate our procedure. However, they do not completely understand our science, and place the needles in an improper fashion. There is no medical basis for such placement of the needles in these men. I know just whose slovenly work this is. His name is Richard Butler. He identifies himself as a practitioner of Oriental medicine and claims the title doctor. However, he is a fraud and would be stopped if we had an appropriate certifying body that was recognized by the British medical authorities. We do have a guild that has stringent requirements for membership, but Mr. Butler would never pass the examination."

As we discussed steps to counter further activities that we could pursue, we were pleased to see Sherlock Holmes reemerge into our group. After getting a briefing from Dr. Huang, Holmes said, "We will need to find and follow Richard Butler to see if he intends to harm any additional victims. We will also need to surviel the betting parlor in the morning to determine what their input would be."

The following evening, Holmes and I waited in the cold mist outside the medical facility of Richard Butler. It was truly a chilly time lag. Finally, a well dressed bearded man appeared in the dim light. He was attired in an expensively-tailored wool coat with a rich fur collar and cuffs on his sleeves. In his hand was displayed a walking stick weighted with a round metal ball. He was obviously successful and prepared for the dangerous men that he sometimes dealt with.

Wearing soundless canvas tennis shoes, Holmes and I followed him at a distance of at least 20 feet and stayed in the darkness, avoiding the lights on the street corners and in the several buildings. Eventually, his path led to a well known boxing gymnasium, in the neighborhood of the betting parlor. The odor was reminiscent of a prize-fighting establishment – a mixture of dried blood and sweat. Before Holmes and I followed the bogus doctor inside, I overheard two seedily dressed men of the street addressing him. After the three men entered, the pair handed him several gold coins, and pointed out two Chinese men lying nude and recumbent on the floor. The last thing I remembered that evening was when Holmes turned the corner of the room to follow Mr. Butler and the men carrying his victims. However, I was distracted by two loiterers playing a game of pocket billiards and lost track of Holmes. Before I could follow him, the back of my head was met with a hard object and the sweetly sickening odor of chloroform penetrated my nostrils.

When I finally resumed consciousness, I was lying on my back on a soft bed in a darkened room. I saw a blonde-haired goddess stroking my bare chest and saying "Dr. Watson, please wake up."

As I slowly returned to my senses, I realized that I was being ministered to by Maurice's beautiful wife, and that I had not yet arisen to heaven.

Jeanine lifted her head and called for Maurice while I blushed that she should have seen me naked. Seeing my unease, she covered me in a clean sheet.

Maurice entered the bedroom that I was lying in and smiled. He said, "James, we were quite worried about you. When Sherlock found you in the alley, you had been rendered insensitive. You were disabled with an obvious blow to the back of your cranium and knocked out with chloroform. Your abdomen had been penetrated with very thin needles in a now familiar pattern. We have extracted them for examination and thoroughly cleansed the spots with saponified creosol. For some reason, you did not suffer from tetanus. I have a theory that your work in the laboratory immunized you against that microbe."

I groggily responded, "Did you apprehend the villain? What were they up to?"

From the doorway, Holmes responded, "Yes, we caught them. The gamblers revealed, under intense interrogation, that they had placed very large bets on the British team in the upcoming Rugby tournament. When they read about the excellent proficiency of the all-star group from Hong Kong, they realized that they needed to change the odds. Thus, they thought that their clever method of murder would obfuscate their means of assassination. Fortunately, the team of Watson and Verner were on the job. I'm sorry that I didn't keep an eye on you when I turned the corner. The so-called doctor and his associates must have recognized you from the drawings by in your published stories, and realized that you were on their trail."

I asked, "What has been the fate of the men who accosted me?"

Maurice replied, "Mr. Phelps and two very burly comrades took the doctor and his colleagues away. They are now, no doubt, tenants of a secret government location, never to be seen again."

Then Holmes added, "The manager of the Chinese rugby team was very grateful. He will be receiving substitute players for the game. As a reward, we have been granted first class tickets to the match and a party afterwards. Perhaps you will enlighten me about the finer points of a game that you are experienced in. As you know, I have never been an aficionado of team sports."

Then, as we sat around the table with our customary drinks and cigars, Verner made an announcement. "James, I was highly pleased that you did not succumb to tetanus. I'm certain that our quick retrieval of the contaminated needles was useful, as was the decontaminant wash. Also, however, I think that your work in the laboratory with these microbes may have provided an immunological resistance. A pharmaceutical company in Detroit, Michigan, in America has begun studies to provide a vaccine to prevent tetanus and an active antiserum to salvage the life of injured people. My uncle Horace Vernet has already set up a facility in several warehouses on the strait between that city and Ontario, in Canada. I will join him to continue my bacteriological research with the financial assistance of the drug company. We will, of course, pursue other business ventures in that booming metropolis."

This announcement saddened me. I was losing one of my only close friends. Perhaps someday I will have the opportunity to visit his American facilities in the future.

Also from MX Publishing

MX Publishing is the world's largest specialist Sherlock Holmes publisher, with over a hundred titles and fifty authors creating the latest in Sherlock Holmes fiction and non-fiction.

From traditional short stories and novels to travel guides and quiz books, MX Publishing cater for all Holmes fans.

The collection includes leading titles such as *Benedict Cumberbatch In Transition* and *The Norwood Author* which won the 2011 Howlett Award (Sherlock Holmes Book of the Year).

MX Publishing also has one of the largest communities of Holmes fans on Facebook with regular contributions from dozens of authors.

www.mxpublishing.com

Also from MX Publishing

Our bestselling books are our short story collections;

'Lost Stories of Sherlock Holmes' , 'The Outstanding Mysteries of Sherlock Holmes', The Papers of Sherlock Holmes Volume 1 and 2, 'Untold Adventures of Sherlock Holmes' (and the sequel 'Studies in Legacy) and 'Sherlock Holmes in Pursuit', 'The Cotswold Werewolf and Other Stories of Sherlock Holmes' – and many more......

www.mxpublishing.com

Also from MX Publishing

"Phil Growick's, 'The Secret Journal of Dr Watson', is an adventure which takes place in the latter part of Holmes and Watson's lives. They are entrusted by HM Government (although not officially) and the King no less to undertake a rescue mission to save the Romanovs, Russia's Royal family from a grisly end at the hand of the Bolsheviks. There is a wealth of detail in the story but not so much as would detract us from the enjoyment of the story. Espionage, counter-espionage, the ace of spies himself, double-agents, double-crossers...all these flit across the pages in a realistic and exciting way. All the characters are extremely well-drawn and Mr Growick, most importantly, does not falter with a very good ear for Holmesian dialogue indeed. Highly recommended. A five-star effort."
The Baker Street Society

www.mxpublishing.com

Also from MX Publishing

The Missing Authors Series

Sherlock Holmes and The Adventure of The Grinning Cat
Sherlock Holmes and The Nautilus Adventure
Sherlock Holmes and The Round Table Adventure

"Joseph Svec, III is brilliant in entwining two endearing and enduring classics of literature, blending the factual with the fantastical; the playful with the pensive; and the mischievous with the mysterious. We shall, all of us young and old, benefit with a cup of tea, a tranquil afternoon, and a copy of Sherlock Holmes, The Adventure of the Grinning Cat."
Amador County Holmes Hounds Sherlockian Society

www.mxpublishing.com

Also from MX Publishing

The American Literati Series

The Final Page of Baker Street
The Baron of Brede Place
Seventeen Minutes To Baker Street

"The really amazing thing about this book is the author's ability to call up the 'essence' of both the Baker Street 'digs' of Holmes and Watson as well as that of the 'mean streets' of Marlowe's Los Angeles. Although none of the action takes place in either place, Holmes and Watson share a sense of camaraderie and self-confidence in facing threats and problems that also pervades many of the later tales in the Canon. Following their conversations and banter is a return to Edwardian England and its certainties and hope for the future. This is definitely the world before The Great War."
Philip K Jones

www.mxpublishing.com

Also from MX Publishing

The Detective and The Woman Series

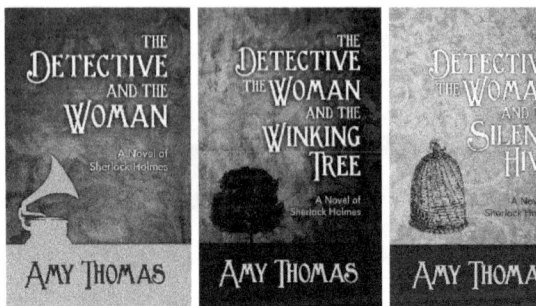

The Detective and The Woman
The Detective, The Woman and The Winking Tree
The Detective, The Woman and The Silent Hive

"The book is entertaining, puzzling and a lot of fun. I believe the author has hit on the only type of long-term relationship possible for Sherlock Holmes and Irene Adler. The details of the narrative only add force to the romantic defects we expect in both of them and their growth and development are truly marvelous to watch. This is not a love story. Instead, it is a coming-of-age tale starring two of our favorite characters."
Philip K Jones

www.mxpublishing.com

Also from MX Publishing

The Sherlock Holmes and Enoch Hale Series

The Amateur Executioner
The Poisoned Penman
The Egyptian Curse

"The Amateur Executioner: Enoch Hale Meets Sherlock Holmes", the first collaboration between Dan Andriacco and Kieran McMullen, concerns the possibility of a Fenian attack in London. Hale, a native Bostonian, is a reporter for London's Central News Syndicate - where, in 1920, Horace Harker is still a familiar figure, though far from revered. "The Amateur Executioner" takes us into an ambiguous and murky world where right and wrong aren't always distinguishable. I look forward to reading more about Enoch Hale."
Sherlock Holmes Society of London

Also from MX Publishing

Sherlock Holmes novellas in verse

All four novellas have been released also in audio format with narration by Steve White

Sherlock Holmes and The Menacing Moors
Sherlock Holmes and The Menacing Metropolis
Sherlock Holmes and The Menacing Melbournian
Sherlock Holmes and The Menacing Monk

"The story is really good and the Herculean effort it must have been to write it all in verse—well, my hat is off to you, Mr. Allan Mitchell! I wouldn't dream of seeing such work get less than five plus stars from me…" **The Raven**

Also from MX Publishing

When the papal apartments are burgled in 1901, Sherlock Holmes is summoned to Rome by Pope Leo XII. After learning from the pontiff that several priceless cameos that could prove compromising to the church, and perhaps determine the future of the newly unified Italy, have been stolen, Holmes is asked to recover them. In a parallel story, Michelangelo, the toast of Rome in 1501 after the unveiling of his Pieta, is commissioned by Pope Alexander VI, the last of the Borgia pontiffs, with creating the cameos that will bedevil Holmes and the papacy four centuries later. For fans of Conan Doyle's immortal detective, the game is always afoot. However, the great detective has never encountered an adversary quite like the one with whom he crosses swords in "The Vatican Cameos.."

"An extravagantly imagined and beautifully written Holmes story"
(**Lee Child**, NY Times Bestselling author, Jack Reacher series)

www.ingramcontent.com/pod-product-compliance
Lightning Source LLC
Chambersburg PA
CBHW060749180626

46818CB00002B/518